More Praise for

NEWS FROM THE
WORLD

"[Fox's] voice is strikingly mature. A writer's job, she implies in the preface to this collection, is to take a 'living interest in all living creatures,' and these pieces attest to her brilliant success at that task." —*The Atlantic*

"Paula Fox's essays and short stories all display a spare, marvelous luminosity. The author's irreducible voice—it was the same with Virginia Woolf—can always be heard, whatever the genre."
—Thomas Mallon, author of *Watergate: A Novel*

"Deeply contemplative and disarmingly courageous, Fox's work astonishes readers with its lucidity." —Carol Haggas, *Booklist*

"A careful glimpse into Fox's working processes, where the correspondences between varied modes provide a study of the relationship between art and life, of the way one experience can be pursued to divergent ends by different genres."
—Stephen Burn, *Bookforum*

"Paula Fox is one of our greatest writers. Her prose is a model of ruthless, gorgeous efficiency, and her mind is so unnervingly alert to the messy contradictions that come with being human. These essays and stories will delight and inspire anyone who cares about literature, storytelling, and truth itself."

—Tom Bissell, author of *The Father of All Things*

"Fox writes like she's living and we just happened to show up and watch. . . . To read Fox's words is to sit at her feet, to take part in what feels at times like oral tradition rather than a more scholarly mode of writing. As the stories and essays unfold in reverse chronological order, the reader becomes increasingly attuned to Fox's particular manner." —Sarah Terez Rosenblum, *Pop Matters*

"The short stories are sparely written with great economy of language while conveying the great truths of life in love, death, loneliness, and happiness. . . . *News from the World* is a 'must read' for all of [Fox's] loyal readers and is a great introduction to her gift for giving the world its 'news' in descriptive but economical language." —Sandra Clariday, Tennessee Library Association

"Paula Fox's essays and short stories in this new compilation range wide and deep; that is, an essay will travel some ground, deposit ideas, make some assertions before coming to rest. Her gorgeous sentences—empty of excess—support complicated emotions, build multiple layers of story and take us to surprising intersections where associations take on meaning."

—Rae Francoeur, *Wicked Local*

NEWS FROM THE
WORLD

ALSO BY PAULA FOX

MEMOIRS

Borrowed Finery

The Coldest Winter: A Stringer in Liberated Europe

NOVELS

Desperate Characters

The God of Nightmares

Poor George

A Servant's Tale

The Western Coast

The Widow's Children

NEWS FROM THE WORLD

Stories and Essays

Paula Fox

W. W. NORTON & COMPANY
NEW YORK • LONDON

"The Living" and "Lord Randal" courtesy of Johnson
Publishing Company, Inc. All rights reserved.

For information about permission to reproduce
selections from this book, write to Permissions,
W. W. Norton & Company, Inc.,
500 Fifth Avenue, New York, NY 10110

For information about special discounts for bulk
purchases, please contact W. W. Norton Special Sales
at specialsales@wwnorton.com or 800-233-4830

Manufacturing by RR Donnelley, Harrisonburg
Book design by Ellen Cipriano
Production manager: Julia Druskin

Library of Congress Cataloging-in-Publication Data

Fox, Paula.
News from the world : stories and essays /
Paula Fox. — 1st ed.
p. cm.
ISBN 978-0-393-08128-2 (hardcover)
I. Title.
PS3556.O94N49 2011
813'.54—dc22
2010047422

ISBN 978-0-393-34234-5 pbk.

W. W. Norton & Company, Inc.
500 Fifth Avenue, New York, N.Y. 10110
www.wwnorton.com

W. W. Norton & Company Ltd.
Castle House, 75/76 Wells Street, London W1T 3QT

1 2 3 4 5 6 7 8 9 0

I thank my husband, Martin Greenberg, not only for his technical help but for his encouragement of my work for forty-eight years.

And to the memory of Pat O'Donnell and Mary King.

CONTENTS

PREFACE

MY FATHER, PAUL HERVEY FOX, was a writer and a drunk. When he was nineteen, he sold his first short story to *Smart Set*. H. L. Mencken, the well-known editor of the magazine, invited him to lunch at a famous restaurant of the period, Delmonico's. My father told me he had been too overwhelmed, too excited, to order anything more elaborate than scrambled eggs.

Paul wrote plays in the 1920s, and one of them, *Soldiers and Women*, ran for just under a year and led to an offer from a Hollywood studio. He went out west to become a screenwriter. He began to drink on the first day of work and continued consuming alcohol for over a year. A fellow screenwriter was concerned; he drove my father, slouched over in an alcoholic stupor in the passenger seat, to the Mojave Desert and left him alone with a table, a typewriter, a cot, and a barrel of drinking water. Paul began his first novel there, *Sailor Town*. A New York publisher took it. After its publication, he left Hollywood and wrote a few more novels with periods of alcoholic indulgence in between the books he produced.

He was married twice, once to my mother, Elsie, and then to Mary with whom he had four children.

On the few occasions I saw my father during my childhood and adolescence, he was drunk most of the time. As a young man he had been handsome. His voice, poetic and slurred, was given over to interminable, stumbling descriptions of the ways in which he and fellow writers tried to elude domesticity and women. All writers, he asserted, were defeated romantics, trying to escape domesticity and females to aspire upward to the mountain heights, only to be dragged down to the lowlands by the female urgencies of breeding and nesting.

I couldn't help myself from imagining mountain slopes covered with writers crawling upward toward the peaks.

When I moved to New Orleans soon after December 7, 1941, Pearl Harbor, and the U.S. precipitation into World War II, I found a clerking job in a government office on the shore of Lake Pontchartrain. My first landlady in the French Quarter was a middle-aged actress who was, like my father, an alcoholic. After a few tumultuous weeks with her, I moved into a tiny room over a kitchen in a building owned by two writers, Mary King and Pat O'Donnel.

Pat had been employed by a Biloxi factory making machine parts. Sherwood Anderson, the writer, stopped by one day to be shown around the premises, and Pat was chosen by the management to be his guide. At the end of an hour's tour during which Anderson listened to Pat explaining the functions and products of various machines, Anderson said to him, "You ought to be a writer."

Pat moved into the Quarter and began his first novel, *Green Margins*, advertising in the local newspaper for a typist. Mary King was about to return to her family in east Texas that very day. At once she was typing away at his novel, which went on to win the Houghton Mifflin award for a first novel. Meanwhile they had fallen in love and moved into a small house on St. Ann Street. Mary was a writer too. Her first novel, *Quincy Bolivar*, won in turn the same Houghton Mifflin award.

Everything about them was contrary to what I had absorbed—as if it had been a religion—from my father. Their goodness, their sobriety, the seriousness with which they worked, their welcoming sweetness of being, their high sense of the comic in life, were in stark contrast to Paul Fox's lack of seriousness.

This collection of stories and essays is dedicated to Pat and Mary, who taught me by example a living interest in all living creatures.

NEWS FROM THE WORLD

CIGARETTE

WHEN I WAS eleven, I spent a few autumn months in an old wooden house with flaking yellow interior walls that stood a few hundred feet or so from the shore of the St. John's River in East Jacksonville, Florida.

On weekday mornings, I walked through a small woods of scrubby pine trees to a narrow blacktop road where I was picked up by a bus and, along with other children, driven to the local public school. When I returned home, I was met at the door by an elderly Scot housekeeper, Mrs. Lesser. She was the mother of a college friend of Mary's. Mary, the owner of the house, was a young woman of means who was going to marry my father once his divorce from Elsie, my mother, was final.

On hot afternoons I would go for a swim in the St. John's River. My jumping-off place was one side of a decayed gray dock that rested on splintery posts. I would jump up and down on the rotting planks until four or five water moccasins, poisonous snakes, slithered down the posts and dropped in thick tangles into the river. Mattie, a boy my age and a friend who lived nearby on the river, instructed me in how to do this.

At the beginning of my stay in the old house, a variety of people, mostly relatives, came to occupy its barely furnished rooms: my father alone for a few days, then my mother for a few days, then her mother—my Spanish grandmother—for a week, then Mary, whom I met there for the first time. She didn't look at me as she pushed a book in my direction. I took it because I had to. It was a collection of short stories by Katherine Mansfield. There was a moment of uncertainty between us. "Keep it . . . ," she muttered faintly.

I didn't know my parents well at all. I had not lived with them. But what I did know was that all the adults who stayed so briefly in the old house were lying to each other as well as to me—except for old Mrs. Lesser, who didn't say much of anything.

As I jumped up and down on the planks of the dock, I found it a relief, a scary relief, to watch the snakes slide down the posts and into floating patches of water hyacinths, their mottled, gray, warty heads poking out from amid the delicate white blossoms and thick green leaves—so substantial, so plainly what they were.

My father spoke in elaborate metaphors to convey, or conceal, what he meant. I couldn't tell the difference. Or else he talked with comic exaggeration; just underneath his words I heard a note of melancholy.

Halfway between the wooden house and the shores of the river ran an embankment about thirty feet high. On a pebble-strewn path stood several iron benches. My father asked me to meet him there one afternoon. I was relieved it was a Saturday. He might have seen my going to school as an evasion.

We had eaten a late lunch prepared by Mrs. Lesser. I was aware that my mother, Elsie, kept her face turned away from me as a I cast frequent, fearful glances at her.

Daddy was waiting for me on the path, sitting on one of the benches, his long legs stretched out in front of him, his hands in his pockets. In the second before I called out to him, I looked openly at his face. There was no expression on it. It was as though he was waiting for someone to come along to bring him into life.

As soon as he saw me, he sat up and seized me by the shoulders. "I know you're smoking behind my back, you little rat! I smelled tobacco on your breath! Here! Take these!" And he thrust an open pack of cigarettes into my right hand.

After so many decades, I can still see the bench, the path, the broad river below, the yellow camel depicted on the pack.

He forced my fingers to close on the pack. "Now you'll be honest!" he said. "Now you'll smoke in front of me!"

In his hand he held a bent cigarette. Suddenly, he grabbed my head with one hand, at the same time pushing the cigarette between my lips. "There!" he exclaimed triumphantly. "Smoke it while we have an erudite conversation!"

He clasped his hands behind his head as he leaned back against the bench. He said, "Amuse me, my child . . ." But, I couldn't answer him; I was choking on the first drag of the cigarette he had lit with a blue-tipped match.

I smoked for decades, through marriages, the births of my children, the writing of my books.

One day, after years of warning about the dangers of tobacco, I joined, halfheartedly, an anti-smoking group, then another and then another. The lecturers who exhorted us to stop were similar in their approach to the problems of quitting, no matter what their age or gender. Often, they clasped their hands in front of them and smiled knowingly as they spoke with professional enthusiasm of the benefits and blessings of quitting.

In one of the groups I especially noticed a woman in a wheelchair, an oxygen tube clamped to one arm, smoking avidly with her free hand, a doomed expression on her face.

Once I was able to stop for almost a year. Then I won a literary prize and had to travel from Manhattan, where I lived, to Chicago, to receive it. I stayed at a posh hotel on the shores of Lake Michigan in a large room that came with the prize.

I wondered if there was someone I knew in that city. I opened the desk drawer to search for a telephone directory that I assumed was there. Instead, I found a narrow, elongated box.

I opened it. Lying side by side were three long thin cigarettes, my name printed on them in gold letters.

I smoked them all. I was off again. I gave up giving up.

⌐~⌐

In 1996, my husband, Martin, and I flew to Israel to spend a month in Jerusalem where we both had fellowships at a scholars' and artists' residence. Our plane landed at Ben Gurion Airport, where we took a taxi to Jerusalem and the residence.

It was a Friday, a day of religious observance. There was no one at the desk of the residence to summon a porter for our luggage. After a while a man, who looked like a janitor in a New York City housing project, appeared. He duly checked our passports and carried our bags up to our quarters, to our surprise a handsome duplex looking across a valley down to the great white wall girdling the Old City.

As we were putting our clothes away, Ilana, Irving Howe's widow and an Israeli citizen, knocked on the door. We were happy to see her, swept aside her excuses for not meeting our plane as had been planned. We had a great deal to talk about and there was the fruit from the large basket she bore to taste. We sat around the living room table until dark. I turned on a lamp and we all talked some more.

It was late by the time we left the residence. Ilana recalled a non-kosher restaurant in the vicinity. The streets were empty, strange. The restaurant was beneath the street level, a kind of cave with many stone steps leading down to it. The place was crowded and noisy. You could walk out of it straight into a connecting movie house. I ordered something. It was revolting, a mess with slices of potato, dressed in a sauce made of axle grease, or so I imagined.

We climbed up the steps and began to walk along a bush-backed stony path that led to the residence. I paused to look some distance down at the brilliantly lit wall of David. Every building around it was bathed in a golden light like ships on a dark sea.

As I turned back to the path, Martin and Ilana talking animatedly a few steps behind me, a hunched figure on a shadowy bench suddenly unwound its length and sprang at me, knocked me to the ground as he wrenched out of my hands my beige canvas bag that held credit cards, passport and dollars, and made off into the darkness.

I vanished into unconsciousness, into nowhere, nothingness. I learned long after that Martin had started after the attacker, then turned back to me. Ilana had run frantically down the path, soon finding a couple with a cell phone who at once called the police.

I was taken by ambulance to the Hadassah Hospital. I had regained consciousness. After an examination the doctor in charge of the emergency room decided that I should be kept overnight. Martin and Ilana returned to the residence. The next morning Ilana phoned the hospital and was told that my condition had unexpectedly worsened in the night. I was diagnosed as having intracranial bleeding and removed, unconscious, to Intensive Care.

A hard spray of water directed at me by a nurse as I slumped on a closed toilet seat in a bathroom with a tiled floor was my awakening into limited consciousness. I appreciated the unorthodox bath but not much else. I didn't know what day it was. I was paralyzed on my right side and speechless. I tried to speak but dribbled meaningless sounds.

I learned subsequently that Martin and Professor Umansky,

the chief of Neurology, had stepped aside into a corner where the professor said, "No surgery. It's worse than the wound." Martin, shocked that there had been such a possibility, was silent with relief. All about the Neurology section were patients with lumpy, large, cruel-looking bandages on their heads.

Meanwhile, my two sons and daughter had come to Jerusalem from the different parts of the United States where they lived. I had lost so much weight so quickly, so much color, that they walked right past me without recognition, as I was huddled in a wheelchair.

Gradually, thoughts, feelings, words leaked drop by drop into my brain. I smiled at nurses, doctors, other patients as an infant smiles, making no distinction. A middle-aged woman, a patient, was being discharged to go home. Martin said she had invited me to visit her when I got out of the hospital. I nodded at her, smiling.

I was wheeled to a window that looked out on the Judean Hills. A light sparkled far off in the ancient, ancient hills. I imagined it was Ali Baba's cave. A nurse told me it was a pane of glass in a garage door.

I wasn't in pain. I gradually learned to say Thank You. Yes. No.

On the first day that I was allowed to go outside, my eldest son, Adam, wheeled me into the elevator and through the lobby, where we passed what seemed a crowd of people but was a large Arab family pressed close together, their bodies massive looking because of their tribal dress. The men were in deep conversation, the women silent, their heads up and waiting like birds in a nest.

Our objective—not mine, really, for I was living in a present free of all objectives—was the Marc Chagall Hospital chapel, whose windows had been painted by the master.

I stared at the world around me: the high vertical walls of the hospital that seemed to rise up before us as we progressed, the petal-flecked beds of flowers growing in irregular patches all around the cement path we followed, the smell of the flowers in the air, an enormous garage beneath the ground nearby where I saw ambulances parked, the swinging doors of the hospital when we returned.

I was started on therapy. I only half-comprehended why I was made to contend with a huge refractory rubber ball among other perverse contraptions. Once Martin was wheeling me to the therapy room when we came to an abrupt halt at the intersection of two corridors. Three doctors were bent over an Israeli soldier still in uniform on a gurney, his face and torso shielded by basket-like metal contrivances. One naked foot hung lifelessly from the end of the gurney. He had died at the intersection. I knew in a single swoop of awareness that I was in Israel.

On Fridays there were no personnel to run the elevators. Adam operated one to the first floor so I could have what had become my daily outing. But what I really liked was wheeling myself to the windows on my floor and looking out upon the Judean Hills.

On the last day but one of my stay at the Hadassah, two large policemen came to question me. Linda, my daughter, was at my side. I stammered and stumbled in attempting to answer their questions about the assault. I knew nothing, only what I had heard others say. I was required to sign papers; I made what seemed to me to be endless circles on the paper, pressing the pen point hard. When I saw what I had done, I smiled apologetically.

The next night we were driven to Ben Gurion Airport to board an airplane that would fly us to New York. Ben Gurion looked to me like a vast exhibition hall. Ilana was there to say goodbye; she was staying on in Tel Aviv a few more days. We passed trunks, drifting people. The ceiling was so high! I felt suddenly alarmed, razor cuts of nameless anxiety. Ilana looked at my hands as they gripped the wheelchair arms. "It will be all right," she said over and over. What was *it*?

I was chairlifted into the airplane, then carried down the aisle by Linda and Gabe, my younger son, to my seat. Next to me sat Martin. Everywhere in the airplane there was a crush of people.

Adam, who had gone ahead to New York a few days earlier, was to meet us at Kennedy Airport. In a wheelchair, I was the last to leave the airplane, preceded by what seemed an escort of bearded young men wearing hats. Hasidic Jews, Martin told me days later.

Adam drove us to the Columbia Presbyterian Hospital, where I was to spend another week. As I was wheeled through the lobby, I felt I was about to faint from fatigue.

I found myself in a large room. A silent nurse dressed me in hospital attire. I noted there was a bathroom with a shower. As soon as I felt the touch of sheets, I fell asleep. At some point an aide woke me. She was standing across the room looking down at a little wheeled table. Why, she asked, in an admonitory voice, hadn't I marked down what I wanted for supper on the menu she was holding up? "I—" I began but was unable to go on. She left the room, casting a dark look at me as she went.

I made a decision then, the first one I had ever made, it seemed to me. I would take a shower. I walked fast—to overcome my unsteadiness—to the bathroom and turned on the taps, letting the water wash over me, not bothering with cloth or soap. It was a taste of freedom, those two minutes or so while I stood there, not aware of the water temperature or anything else except that it seemed the first choice of my life.

On a weekend day, I was wheeled to the lower floor of the hospital by an aide. A young man who seemed drunk told me I was going to have a CAT scan. I was instantly terrified—by the thought of claustrophobia. But he laughed and told me I would suffer nothing of the kind. And it turned out to be so—a sliding in and a sliding out.

Our Dr. McCormick came to visit me. I was glad to see him, explained I'd had an accident in Havana, Cuba, realized at once the error I had made and apologized to him. He smiled amiably and said, "I'm used to it," meaning, I thought, states of confusion.

Martin drove us home to Brooklyn five days later. I looked intently out of the car window at the traffic, the buildings, buses like bumblebees, people's faces in car windows bent over the steering wheels, or blank-faced passengers staring straight ahead. Out of some faces poked white narrow tubes. Cigarettes. I smelt (I suppose I imagined) cigarette smoke. I felt revulsion—to my astonishment. Till that moment the thought or the wish to smoke hadn't crossed my mind. I realized I had lost any impulse to light up. We were home. I was helped up the stairs and went right to bed.

The next day I woke up feeling an obligation to finish all the medicine I had been given in vials and boxes. I couldn't read, for months it seemed. I couldn't speak directly about anything; I avoided subjects as if they'd been land mines. I wandered around my room like a doleful animal and spoke like one, painfully aware of my speech as being nearly without meaning yet unable to be silent, and singularly conscious of the mess I was in.

I spent over a month in bed. Except for trips to the bathroom next door, my life was without sense. Friends visited with flowers. Often they wept, staring down at me.

One day I ventured down the stairs and surprised Martin and Gabe in the kitchen. I looked at the stove and the refrigerator as they scolded and congratulated me.

I managed the stairs with more and more confidence and spent a few moments of each day with my friend Sheila who lives next door. I heard myself stammer and stumble and blunder.

A look at the *Times* and I found I could read. A book about the human brain was hard going. All I recall was a case about a composer who had been assaulted on a street in Paris. When he regained his physical strength he discovered he could no longer read music. I began to read Trollope's novels.

The time came for me to see a neurologist, Dr. Robert E. Barrett, whom Martin often and I a little had gone to for years. By then I had started a memoir. It took me three months to write nine pages.

The brain is an organ of endlessly changing borders. It is so unknown. Yet when some function is gone, we are likely to know it at once. In my case, after the Jerusalem assault, it was the geometry of the house I had lived in until I was six years old that I could no longer reconstruct in memory.

I couldn't explain or write about the relation of the attic stairs to a narrow corridor that passed a bedroom on the way to a staircase that led to the kitchen below.

I told Dr. Barrett that I no longer had the least desire to smoke cigarettes.

Dr. Barrett was a handsome man in his sixties, an engaging, charming conversationalist. I found him easy to talk with despite my trouble with speech. I told him about the assault as well as I could, although I knew that he'd had an earlier report from Martin.

He smiled at me with great tenderness, great sympathy. As I climbed up and down over verbs and over nouns, trying to keep subjects in order, I spoke about my new aversion to tobacco.

The years rolled away like a handful of marbles before my staring eyes. I saw my father's face over mine, his fingers forcing my first cigarette into my mouth.

"That's a hell of a way to quit," Dr. Barrett said.

CLEM

I ACCOMPANIED MARTIN with some timidity to meet my future father-in-law, Joseph Greenberg, in his apartment on Central Park West. He and his wife, Fan, Martin's stepmother, looked at me, I imagined, with some surprise—I wondered what they had expected. Joe brought out a bottle of Chivas Regal. (In all our future visits he would greet me in the same way.) He was a harsh man with an ironical wit; so Martin had described him and so he seemed. But he was cordial enough to me. After a few minutes of awkward greetings, he began to tell stories of his early years in Russo-Poland. Martin said later that his father had told me more about himself than he had ever told him in all the years of his childhood and youth.

It was a different story with Clement Greenberg, my future brother in-law. I met him and Sol, also a brother-in-law-to-be, at an evening party that I had anticipated would be noisy with people talking and drinking and looking me over with curious, perhaps not very friendly eyes. As Martin and I pushed open the door to a flat in an Upper West Side loft building, a man's voice boomed out, "Here, finally, are all three Greenberg brothers!" Whatever that meant, it made me uneasy.

I still find it painful to recall those two or three hours forty-nine years ago and the distress they were filled with for me. I was blind to the presence of other guests. Why was I there, I asked myself with grim self-commiseration, in that big room filled with strangers, flinging their arms and legs about, picking up and setting down drinks, one man carrying a nearly empty bottle of Jack Daniels, some arguing, some whispering? Why had I chosen to wear such a low-necked sweater? I hunched my shoulders so as to hide what the sweater did not.

Curiosity gradually displaced my self-preoccupation. Was something going to happen? Or nothing? I heard sudden loud laughter, Sol's, a rising wave that broke seconds later into soft groans—his characteristic laughter, as I learned over the years. He leaned forward from a chair in the corner, looking at me. Was it me he had been laughing at? My face creased with an automatic smile. He stood up, threading his way among groups of people, some in loud, intense conversations, to reach my side.

"That's a lovely sweater you're wearing," he observed with what seemed to be amusement, as though he had recognized the source of my discomfort. He seemed good-humored. At once I felt that it was false; I suspected him of being clownish rather than tolerant. He showed a faintly affected scorn (or so I imagined later). Perhaps it was for what his younger brother might do next, after turning up with a half-naked woman not his wife.

Over the years I discovered that there were moments of real kindness in him that would flash out suddenly like a beam of sunlight falling on a floor. But not always. I knew there was a fourth Greenberg child, a half-sister, who was not at the party. She was never at such parties—she inhabited a different world.

Sol had been a Trotskyite before World War II. Both his brothers, the oldest and the youngest, had followed him into Trotskyism. In time Martin and Clem turned away from all political ideology, without ceasing to be anti-Stalinist. Sol, however, became a militant neo-con.

In spite of his stony political severity, it was easy for me to make him laugh.

Later in the evening, finally, we encountered Clem, to whom Martin formally introduced me. Martin had spoken of him often, describing him as a brilliant brute. Clem had been twenty-nine when he had published an essay, "Avant-garde and Kitsch," in the *Partisan Review*. It had attracted a great deal of attention and started him on his career as a celebrated—and furiously denounced—art critic. He seemed as much interested in literature as in art. It was clear to me that he knew a great deal.

Clem was nine years older than Martin and had been a forceful, if sometimes cruel, presence for his younger brother during the latter's boyhood and beyond, though Martin's going off to the University of Michigan at sixteen had helped him escape from under his brother's shadow—partly.

When I stood face to face with Clem that evening, I had the

impression that he had more important things to do than converse with me. His voice was indifferent, dismissive, cold. As were his words. I feared him and his judgments. He resembled Martin physically, I saw, but, as was quickly evident, not otherwise. In those few minutes I sensed in him an enormous vitality of interest, as well as an opposing capacity for boredom. His heavy drinking blurred both qualities in his later years.

When he said hello, his lips curled at the corners like two small commas, then his face resumed its indifferent expression. At that moment I thought of a large oil painting he had done, a copy of a nineteenth-century French work, I guessed, that hung on the living-room wall of my future father-in-law's West Side apartment. It depicted a narrow dirt road leading through a thick forest, mostly in shades of blue and green, empty of human figures. Remembering it, its art student's earnestness as I thought, restored an elusive balance for me, as though the painting revealed something hidden about Clem that I couldn't put a name to, and I was able to reply to his hello with a neutral one of my own.

One evening, at a time when I and my two small sons were living in a large apartment on Riverside Drive near Columbia University, I gave a small dinner party. Anxiously, I invited Clem. Martin was there, of course, and a writer friend of mine, James Purdy. During Martin's stint as acting editor of *Commentary* he had published a Purdy story whose appearance in a Jewish magazine had little point, as Martin well knew. A year or so earlier, Martin, after consulting with another editor because he did not trust his own judgment—we had just become acquainted—had turned down one of my own stories as not being suitable for

Commentary. I feel a little pinch of resentment every now and then at having had a story of mine rejected by the man who became my husband.

The evening was stiff, clumsy, but it did not lack talk. What it lacked, perhaps, was mutual curiosity. I served dessert and coffee, after which we repaired to the living room. Clem sat down at once in a big armchair that appears to me in memory as magisterial: because Clem in his husky voice had soon launched out into one authoritative disquisition after another. My nervousness made it difficult for me to follow him. Jim Purdy spoke less, but with his outrageous, often comic contempt for the whole world, especially for other writers. Clem was in the middle of delivering still another pronouncement (I wish I could remember on exactly what); they had become heavier and heavier; then I heard Martin's voice intone, "Yes, Lord." Clem stood up and without looking at anyone left the room. We listened in silence as the front door closed with a bang. Purdy laughed briefly.

Clem had suffered a nervous breakdown after being drafted into the army during World War II and had been given a medical discharge. Martin said he had refused to put up with being in the army; his soul had simply rebelled against it. Martin told me that he rather admired Clem for it. He himself had fitted too well into the army for four and a half long years. Clem had a second breakdown when the two brothers were editors at *Commentary.* Martin and his first wife had taken him into their Great Neck home for quite a while until he recovered.

After we were married, Martin and I usually met Clem, though not often, at my father-in-law's apartment. At our first encounter there, he walked over to me purposefully and, speaking with grim emphasis—obliged, it seemed to me, by his personal, special commitment to speaking truth under all circumstances—declared the ineradicable gratitude he felt toward Martin's first wife. I fell back a step under the admonitory force of his words, shocked. Why would I ever dare to question his feeling of gratitude toward one who had sheltered him? It was his feeling; it had originated long before we had met.

Clem's brief first marriage had produced a son, Danny. His second, to Jenny, lasted, with interruptions, for the rest of his life. They had a daughter, Sara, who now has two children of her own.

Jenny visited us once in Manhattan, mainly, it seemed, to convey Clem's resentment of Martin's apparent neutrality in the war Clem was waging with their father. But Martin seemed hardly neutral to me in his attitude toward his father. I had suggested to him that he try to make some kind of peace with Joe. Fathers and sons notoriously don't get along for many reasons, of which the oedipal one has proven to be of no special importance. A fog obscured the Greenberg battlefield for decades. Joe died at ninety-six. I had found him interesting, often amusing, but the filial visits were, after all, tedious. His sons' struggle with him was hardly affected by his death.

We saw little of either brother during our first years together. In 1963 we traveled on Martin's Guggenheim Fellowship and lived on the island of Thasos off the Thracian coast for six months. I don't remember any correspondence from them. When we returned, Sol had left his painter wife and taken up, as it turned out permanently, with Margaret. She had a large apartment on Fifth Avenue with a grand view of the city, expensively furnished but dull, lacking in individual taste.

On one evening visit I told an anecdote that caused Sol to spill over with laughter throughout the hours afterward. A girl I had heard of at second hand had attended a coeducational boarding school. She went with a boy she had recently met but whom she adored to the school's ice-skating pond. The youth was elegantly provided with two dachshunds, which wandered, sniffing, around. He removed his boots to replace them with ice skates. He was wearing thick brown socks. The girl, searching for some flattering thing to say, came up with: "I like your dogs!" (In those days, *dogs* was a slang word for feet.) Sol exploded. I liked his readiness to laugh, which could dilute his ideological fervor.

We went to dinner at Tavern on the Green in Central Park one evening. Seated at a round table, the four of us talked of many things. Sol spoke harshly—with "let's tell the truth" coldness—about black youths. I replied, "There has to be justice." All his facial tics began to work; for a moment he was transformed into a creature from the Grand Guignol.

He bent his head over his plate and in a low voice said, "You're right."

A few years later I published my fourth novel, *The Western Coast*. It caused trouble with Sol. He telephoned me in Brooklyn, where we had moved. To my hello he responded in a grim, accusatory voice. Part of the novel concerned Communists in California in the 1940s. Sol said, "As if they merited the space you gave them! How could you have written in so mild a tone! What! What!"

Slowly we mended what had been torn between us, returning

to an unquestioning if narrowed trust. He often sat at our Brooklyn dining table of an evening.

Years passed. We rented a house in Maine. Sol was in his seventies. He liked the nickname acquired on the tennis courts of Easthampton, "Ace-bandage Greenberg," bestowed on him by the younger people he played with, for the bandages he wore around his ankles.

One afternoon the phone rang in our Maine rental. Sol was calling from New York. He told Martin that what had been diagnosed earlier as anemia had been determined to be cancer. He died not many months later.

Clem died at the age of eighty-five. He wished, with the counterevidence staring him in the face, to outlive his father's ninety-six years. When I think of him, I see him at a party, drinking and smoking and holding forth. In 1961 he had published a collection of essays, *Art and Culture*, which defined the heart of modern painting as visible on the surface, no deeper than the paint on the canvas. The book represented a historic event in the criticism of art, and he was on his way to becoming famous—something he thought would never happen because of his father's discouraging early influence, and which he never realized had happened.

He went abroad often to lecture. From reports, he was not a fascinating speaker. He was not a man who tried to please. He did not, I feel sure, think that he could please. Defiantly he turned his indifference to pleasing into a refusal to please, into surliness and gracelessness, which he thought a virtue in a world dominated by commercial pleasingness and all the questionable personal smiling. He was sharp about people, but I think he didn't understand

personal relations. He understood himself and he didn't—true of
most of us, I suppose.

We went to see Clem and Jenny off on their way to Europe. It
was in the 1960s, still a time of traveling by ship. Their stateroom
was crowded with people, among them Danny, his son; it was my
first sight of him. He was tall and gaunt, with strawlike reddish hair
covering his head, his look hangdog. His eyes peered guardedly out
from under his brows. A few weeks later, I walked into our living
room to find Danny with my eleven-year-old son, Gabe, and Danny
asking him, "What do you think about sexual intercourse?"

Some years later Danny went to England with a group of
young men, dressed like beggars, who believed they were working to foment world revolution. The English authorities ushered
them out of the country at once. We haven't heard anything about
Danny since.

We were invited by Clem to visit him in his apartment, like
his father's located on Central Park West. A small reason for the
visit was to meet a high Austrian prelate who was interested in
modern art. A man in his fifties, he wore black gaiters on his long,
storklike legs, was narrow-featured and sharp-eyed, and made an
elegant, spidery presence among the ordinary furnishings of the
living room, from whose walls shone down the glittering colors of
paintings by Kenneth Noland, Jules Olitski, and, I think, a small
one by Jackson Pollock. Clem scurried about, bringing water or
wine and an ashtray; his face was strained.

On the subway back to Brooklyn, Martin said he had been
astonished by Clem's obsequious behavior toward the priest.
What was the reason for it, I wondered. The latter acted with the

confidence, touched by hauteur, of a man high in office and in his own estimation—but still, why was Clem as nervous as an altar boy?

While Martin and I had been in Greece with my two boys, my former husband had gotten hold of Clem's unlisted phone number and called him to inquire after his sons' welfare (not usually a pressing concern with him), the implication being that he had not heard from them in months. Clem commented, "His voice was paranoid." I was gratified that he had perceived (I had not spoken a word about my former husband to him) this trait of his nature.

Clem and Jenny visited us briefly at a cottage we rented one summer on Martha's Vineyard. We met them at the island airport, accompanied by Gabriel, then ten. Gabe charmed adults, and Clem was no exception. But it was clear he had no idea of how to behave with children. Again and again from the back seat he exclaimed to Jenny, "Do you notice how attentive he is to us? Did you hear how he expressed his concern for our comfort?" During that visit I invited them to spend New Year's Eve with us in Brooklyn. Jenny's reply, in a vague voice, "Oh, well, you know . . . we go to the same people every year . . . ," reminded me of an earlier occasion when we had met at Joe's apartment and she had referred laughingly to my second novel, *Desperate Characters*, as "Depressing Characters."

We went to Clem's eightieth-birthday party a few years later, in a loft on 23rd Street. There were many guests from all over, and the dust rose from the floorboards chin high. I searched for someone to talk with but had no luck. At the end of one long table covered with glasses was a big chocolate cake. When we left by a corridor that ran by two warehouse elevators, Clem was standing in front of them, his cheeks filled like a squirrel's. I leaned forward to kiss him. He warned me off, saying, "My mouth is stuffed with cake." He said these words with no irritation, indeed cordially.

I never saw the art critic, the family critic, again. He died shortly after giving an interview to the *New York Times* in which his criticism of his father had had an unpleasant tone, making public feelings and opinions he should have kept to himself. The interview suggested the distance at which he held himself from his father and his family. Martin felt that Clem was ashamed of his immigrant Jewish origin. His father spoke with a heavy Yiddish accent.

Clem died in the hospital after a fall in an alcoholic haze after drinking the contents of a bottle of whisky an acquaintance had sneaked past the nurses. Martin visited him there. He was comatose. When he stopped breathing, Martin said good-bye to Jenny and left. When he came home, he was quiet and thoughtful.

For many years now, I've saved a postcard from Clem. (Postcards were what he sent his family and in-laws.) This one, dated 21 December 1984, concerns a novel of mine I had given him.

Dear Paula [it read],
I waited to read A Servant's Tale, before writing to thank you. It's the best ever, I'm glad to say. I started it yesterday & finished it this morning. I couldn't put it down. I'm not saying this to be pleasant or make you feel good. It's a fact, that's all. Luisa evolves and takes me along. I was sorry when the book ended.

Thanks for the inscription. Holiday greetings and love to you both.

Yrs ever,
Clem

I was enormously heartened and pleased, especially because I valued his judgment greatly.

At a memorial held for him in 1995, with no great attendance, Jules Olitski and Clem's daughter Sara spoke. Martin declined. Jules spoke with knowledgeable ease—it was not a conventional eulogy—and humor, too, about Clem's constant refrain, "Pa, Pa, Pa." I have forgotten much, but I do recall how sorry I felt that Clem was dead.

LIGHT ON THE DARK SIDE

ONE MANHATTAN MID-MORNING in the spring of 1967, I heard the crack of a gun going off below, along the broad reach of Central Park West. I jumped up from the table where I was working on my second novel and looked down five stories to the street, on the other side of which breathed the quiet greenery of Central Park. What I saw was a man lying in the middle of the street attempting to raise himself up from the waist, like a seal, collapsing, trying again, then falling flat.

At the same moment that I looked down I saw Billy the doorman glance up at me. We had both witnessed the murder.

Shortly after, two detectives arrived at the door of my apartment. Billy had reported to the police that there was another witness, me.

The detectives drove me to the local precinct on 102nd Street where I was questioned for nearly two hours by a third detective. In the course of the searching interrogation I was led to recall, bit by bit, watching the victim rise up and fall, seeing out of the corner of an eye a green sedan slowly driving by and from a back-seat window an arm thrust out its hand holding a gun and firing a second time.

That evening when Martin, my husband, came home from teaching I reported what I had seen. "Oh God!" he said. "We'll have to move out of here." Later: "Maybe Brooklyn."

I dreaded the long commute such a move would mean for my two sons and me. I had managed to get them full scholarships at the Ethical Culture's school in Riverdale, Fieldston. I taught in Ethical's elementary school located many blocks down Central Park West, at 63rd Street.

The neighborhood we were living in was a slum in the midst of which our apartment house thrust up high in the air like a great watchtower. In the late evenings, hanging out of the bedroom window, I liked to watch what was going on down below on 104th Street. I had once seen, less far down, an elderly woman being mugged on the gravel-strewn roof of a tenement across the way that a century ago had been someone's mansion—a thin youth grabbed her purse, knocked her down, and departed in no great haste, in full view. Often I saw ambulances parking to pick up the wounded or the dead, the vehicles' roofs emblazoned with a red cross. I listened fascinated to drunken conversations echoing upward. So much happened after dark that I began to see the street as a movie set, distance flattening horror as it usually does, turning the suffering of others into a troubling but nevertheless absorbing spectacle.

The Saturday after the shooting, I drove across the Brooklyn Bridge with my younger son. My other boy was visiting schoolmates and Martin was in bed with a virus. I think a friend had told me about Boerum Hill, a small neighborhood in South Brooklyn where, she had heard, there was a three-floor apartment for rent. Or had I seen an ad in a newspaper? What I'm still sure about is the rent: $325 a month, $40 less than we were paying for our apartment on Central Park West.

After several wrong turns, I found Dean Street. Brownstones lined both sides of the narrow street between Hoyt and Bond. A four-story brick hospital rose at the western corner like a bookend. The sidewalks were empty of people. We parked the car with ease; there were many free spaces in those long-ago days.

The sunlight was thin and weak, the air chilly. As I got out of the car, I heard the sound, oddly threatening, of an old window being raised. I looked up to see an old woman staring down at us from the third floor of a house. She slammed the window back down.

The street, the houses on it, had a convalescent, ambiguous look. It wasn't a slum, though it was ragged. It wasn't clearly working-class, it wasn't middle-class (yet). It neither welcomed nor glowered with hostility.

But you saw the sky in a way you rarely saw it in Manhattan. As I looked up at it I realized, as I seldom did in Manhattan, that it was limitless, not a roof for a city, not a part of a stage decor, but the heavens.

We read the house numbers and found the one we wanted, on the north side of the street, close to Bond. The landlord, Ralph, lived in the neighboring house. We climbed up its stoop to the massive door and rang the bell.

A man with a worried expression appeared on the threshold.

"You have a rental available?" I asked. He nodded, turned, and picked up a key from a small table

"Next door. Up the stoop," he said, in a flat voice. "The garden apartment is already rented."

I stared at the dusty windows of the house we were going to inhabit for the next three years.

It looked unsheltered, open to weather, despite being squeezed between adjoining brownstone houses. I had a momentary delusion that it was standing by itself as if on a prairie. Ralph said he owned both houses as he was opening the large entrance door, with a squeak of hinges. I smelled dust. I felt the house's emptiness.

"You're standing in the hallway," Ralph said. "To your right is the living room with kitchen and dining space over there, in the back. The fireplace doesn't work."

The quite large living room was marked by pencil-like shadows cast by the ascending stairs. I noted a thin line of utilities in the rear, all small: sink, stove, refrigerator, two narrow counters. Together they spelled out in a kind of shorthand, *kitchen*. A door at the rear led to the backyard. As I opened it, Ralph said, admonishingly, "Those steps go down to the yard. You can't use them without permission of the tenants below" (who proved to be a quite friendly couple).

We climbed the steps to the next floor. I saw a bathroom, its door open, looking like plain white underwear, slightly soiled. Next to it was a small room with a window giving onto the backyard. I stared into it and the yards of the next street, backed up against those of Dean Street. Dirty windows rebuffed the sun's rays. I could see blurred shapes through some, bedsheets or ragged shades covered others.

On the top floor was another, smaller, bathroom and two rooms, one as large as the living room, the other small.

We returned to Ralph's house where, in his small office, I signed a three-year lease and arranged to move in in two weeks' time. Ralph looked a little less grim as he said, "The utilities are your responsibility, of course."

The evening of the day we moved in, I made a quick supper. We sat at a table surrounded by stacked cartons that evoked in me a memory of Stonehenge, a cardboard one. The atmosphere at our table was a mix of hilarity and malaise. The neighborhood and the house felt alien. We had moved into a foreign city, a feeling shared by some of our friends in Manhattan in those years, and indeed still.

But I was not the first member of my family to live in the borough. My Spanish grandmother, born in Barcelona, married and after a few years widowed in Cuba, turned down her father's offer to pay her passage back to Spain; instead she had sailed for Brooklyn with her five children at the end of the Spanish-American War, in 1898.

She told many stories about the farmhouse in Sterling Place where she and my mother and five uncles had first lived. The neighborhood had been semirural then—she saw tethered goats, chickens scrabbling in the earth of neighboring farms, heard cows mooing. Long ago Sterling Place became a black ghetto.

Gradually I remembered that I had disliked Brooklyn as a child; its shaking, rattling trolleys that seemed to be everywhere in the borough when I rode them to visit my grandmother's friends; its different neighborhoods so dull and ugly, as shabby and discouraging as the suburban Queens we moved to later, as common as I was inclined to feel the whole world was. I was thinking about that as Martin and I and the boys ate our dessert of ice cream that first evening among the packed boxes.

I still felt anxious about my children having to travel the far distance north to Riverdale by subway and bus. I was in a state of worrying indecision about my job at the Ethical Culture school in Manhattan. I had published one novel and begun a second. Time was my trouble. I stretched it, bent it, cursed and tricked it but it still maintained its tyranny. I only relaxed when I sank into bed at night in Boerum Hill.

But I discovered something in the passing weeks and months, the singularity, the charm of the borough: its tree-lined streets and gardens, its distinctive neighborhoods that sometimes changed by the block, and then changed in a different way when the old working-class or slum populations moved out and new ones (from all over the U. S. and Europe too) moved in; young people, house-mad, scraping paint off marble fireplaces and mahogany bannisters, overjoyed to leave asphalt Manhattan behind for what was, most importantly for some, an investment, for some a true dwelling, as true as a dwelling can be in a country, in a world, that shifts and slides as if on sand.

Three years elapsed and we bought a twelve-foot-wide house in a nearby neighborhood west of Dean Street. Down its side streets you could glimpse the Upper Bay. I had finished my second novel and it was duly published. A movie actress bought it as a vehicle for herself—a small-budget film that Frank Gilroy wrote the script for and directed. That made possible our buying and renovating the Rumpelstiltskin house with its waste backyard that had once been a garden and would be so again.

The day before we moved out of Dean Street, I was at my desk in the room I used to write in. Suddenly the window shattered, there was a tremor in the air, a bee-like buzzing flying past my cheek. I shrank with fear. Then collecting myself, I peered out of the window into the backyards. A young man and woman, their hands raised in fright to their faces, were searching in my direction for the broken window. A gun was dangling from the girl's right hand.

It turned out that the foolish young man had been teaching his foolish girlfriend how to fire a gun. He had held it for her as she gripped the butt and was curling her finger around the trigger. It went off.

Again a gun had written *finis* to one of our sojourns. And almost to me. Martin had said more than once that I was a perilous voyager.

◞   ◞

On Dean Street, at its western end at Hoyt, lived L. J. Davis and family, into whose house the future author of *A Meaningful Life* had put time, labor, skill, taste, and lots of money (I presumed) to make it habitable and beautiful even as he wrote his novels, one of which was *Cowboys Don't Cry*. From his youth in Boise, Idaho, he knew about cowboys at first hand. We gossiped on the street with L.J. and others, went to parties at his place, where the talk was publishing and the guests were writers and literary agents. One hot June Sunday when I was in Philadelphia with my younger son visiting relatives, Martin, alone, began to feel a pain in his gut; it got worse. He called our Manhattan doctor (absent on a summer Sunday), the on-duty doctor (busy elsewhere), three doctors in the phone book (one said, correctly, "kidney stone," another, "call the police"); the police said call a doctor.

Martin thought of L.J. and called him, by which time he was crawling on the floor, dragging the phone after him. Miraculously, L.J. was at home, the only other soul on the planet at home on that hot June afternoon. He came, looked in dismay at Martin on the floor, roused out the ambulance of the small Catholic hospital across the way from his house, and, disconcerted by the loud, incessant animal cries my husband was making, had him carried by ambulance to the hospital.

I remember L.J. as an energetic, voluble man whose interests (and writing) were not at all confined to the literary. He knew a lot about all sorts of things, one of which was finance. His impersonal way of greeting you was to announce without preliminary some remarkable, usually grotesque piece of local news or information.

L.J. was a writer. So was I. Yet he had an aura for me, all writers did, because my rarely present, utterly irresponsible, always laugh-inspiring drunk father had been a writer and for me an illuminated being.

L.J. is a serious comic writer. His novels mingle Groucho Marx, a bit of Noël Coward, and some Theodore Dreiser. Dreiser, for those who have forgotten or never known him, is grim, grim. I add to the mix Louis-Ferdinand Céline's *Voyage au bout de la nuit* (*Voyage to the End of the Night*), a masterpiece of loathing. Davis is not only serious, he is stern. Life is a hard business that we need to think about. But all our thought doesn't keep it from being outrageously grotesque, unsuccessful, ridiculous. If I may bring in another illustration, he is like a novel-writing Buster Keaton.

Lowell Lake is the protagonist of *A Meaningful Life*. Although poor, he managed to get hold of enough money to attend Stanford, where he met his Flatbush-born wife. She, after graduation, wished to live in Berkeley, he, a westerner, in New York. Lowell had thought he would drive a cab and write. (Before that he had wanted to be a cowboy.) "Great!" Betty had said.

> That's just great. I can't tell you how that idea really grabs me. What do you think this is? *The Jackie Gleason Show?*

. . . I have to travel three thousand miles and work my ass off for four years in order to marry a New York cab driver? . . . I don't believe it. I've never worn a house dress in my life. At least you could have said you wanted to be a riveter. . . . Riveters make good money and there'd be a nice little pension for me if you walked off a beam up there in the sky. I liked it better when you wanted to be a cowboy.

But New York it was. He tried to write and his wife worked. Finally her uncle Lester got him a job as managing editor of a plumbing-trade monthly magazine. He went to work. "It's about time," said Betty.

The novel opens in Lowell's Manhattan apartment, by now all too familiar, with a certain horror: he gets up early one morning so as "to be out of the room before . . . he had to watch his wife hoist on her girdle and buckle on her bra." Betty, for her part, objects to the way the thin, tall, collapsing Lowell (whose newspaper vendor offers to thin out the Sunday *Times* for him so that it will be easier to carry) sits in his chair. "I hate it when you sit in a chair like that," she says. "What's wrong with the way I'm sitting?" he asks. "It's weak. You're sitting there in a weak way."

His job bores him out of his head. He'd supposed it was temporary; it's going on forever. Then Lowell hears about busy, active people rejuvenating old houses and slums. A drowning man, he reaches for a decayed mansion in a downtown Brooklyn slum to save himself.

Davis is not a writer tender of others' susceptibilities. If you are born in Boise, Idaho, you—that is, Lowell—find two New York minorities (which doesn't seem the right word for them) hard to deal with: his Flatbush Jewish in-laws and the black and Puerto Rican population of the downtown Brooklyn slum he buys into. His mother-in-law looks at him with a "What's this?" expression and never addresses him directly. His short father-in-law always smiles obligingly and tells Lowell to call him Leo. A mild man, he would tell Hitler to call him Leo. He worries about "Negroes"—they are everywhere. Twice a year Lowell and his wife visit his in-laws' plastic-covered apartment for a dinnerless afternoon. He is ignored by the mother, invited by the father to come again to hear the latter's news about "Negroes."

Until he meets his wife's family, people had been

old and calm, the sort of people who made up their lives the same way they made up their beds, neat and clean and tight at the corners and no nonsense about the spread.

Now they had "comic-opera names like Marvin and Irving [and] lived in comic-opera places like Canarsie and Ozone Park."

His wife, who had fled to California to get away from her family, now goes shopping at S. Klein's with her mother and talks to her on the phone about what Lowell calls "a bunch of strangers."

"They're not either strangers," Betty says,

I've known Milly Norinski for years and years. . . . Count yourself lucky that I only talk about her to my mother. Listen, you want me to bore you? Ask me about Milly Norinski one of these times.

Lowell hears her bullying the butcher and fighting with the vegetable man. He can't understand her anymore. She's become a Jekyll-and-Hyde character.

Davis catches Betty's speech exactly. I find her one of the stars of the book, of its Jewish side, though she has only one foot in it; in a petty bourgeois world of a pettiness I suppose real but impossible to conceive. But it is the black and Puerto Rican slum side of *A Meaningful Life* that rolls over and drowns Lowell and the reader in its crashing wave.

The mansion Lowell is going to purchase had been built over the years by a tycoon, a Civil War hero, corporation lawyer, and adventurer. It is "the townhouse of Darius Collingwood, foremost corporation lawyer in the Northeastern United States," so the underage-looking real estate agent impressively names it when husband and wife come to inspect the nearby twenty-one-room Brooklyn structure.

One of the brilliancies of the novel is the biography Davis invents for Darius Collingwood, a parody in the antimacassar style of the late nineteenth century. Collingwood becomes the object of Lowell's intensive research in his quest for the "traditions" he would acquire by purchase.

They survey the property from the street. It is a wreck of "such surpassing opulent hideousness that Lowell could scarcely believe someone was actually offering to sell it to him."

"It's a rooming house," Betty says. "Delivered vacant," says the agent, who compliments her on her knowingness. (Delivered bursting with tenants.)

"What's the C. of O.?" asks his wife. "Class B roomer" is the reply. "Lowell didn't know what they were talking about." Lowell is well done for the novel's purpose, but leaning toward familiar schlemielishness, a hick kind.

At the entrance door, the agent shouts, "Henry! Henry!" Henry opens a window. "Man can't get no sleep," he says. "You can sleep later, Henry. Mr. Grossman wants you to show these people the house now."

"Shee-it! You go tell Mr. Grossman he can goddamn well go and fuck his goddamn self. I ain't no fucking horse. I got to sleep."

Inside they visit unspeakable room after unspeakable room, from turret to cavernous cellar, the floor of which is inundated with a pool of liquid waste leaking from a cracked pipe. Everywhere they encounter rot, ordure, rags, ancient furnishings, broken furniture, torn curtains, ripped window shades, collapsed couches. Different nauseating smells assail them in different rooms.

The tenants are a Beggar's Opera of restless and catatonic, blind and halt, young and old grotesques. Briskly the agent opens a door, without knocking, on a young couple making love. A large Puerto Rican family seated around a large table falls silent, spoons in mid-air while they are being inspected. Lowell, oppressed beyond endurance, declines to return with the agent to his office to "have a chat." They must go back to their apartment. They must shower at once. Lowell must buy the nightmare domicile. He is a mystery to himself.

After one or two roomers are made to depart, the rest flee in a rout, taking with them every object they can lift. Lowell buys tools and embarks on his voyage toward a meaningful life. His power drill is stolen on his first working day. Betty and he labor at cleaning up the rooming house filth and demolishing landlord and tenant additions. He drinks more and more. Betty departs for Flatbush and her mother.

Lowell hires a builder, Cyril P. Busterboy, who laughs "melodiously" when Lowell shows him the "rotten main beam."

"Do you realize that this house used to belong to Darius Collingwood?" he asks Mr. Busterboy. "No shit," the latter replies, and takes a nip from the half-pint of J&B in his back pocket.

Mr. Busterboy, a melodious laugher throughout the renovation, is a pleasant man, the only such in the novel. Davis's comedy is exact and cruel. He sees with a Dickensian eye but never with a slant of vision rightward toward the grotesque-endearing, only leftward toward the grotesque-repellent.

A fellow renovator in a business suit stops by and casts an unfriendly dead look at Lowell's efforts. He says nothing. He leaves. It's a small episode, but peculiarly awful.

Lowell gets ever more drunk. He sleeps over one time, drunk and dreaming, and is wakened in the middle of the night. Terrified, he picks up a crowbar and smashes the intruder's head, disposes of the body in Mr. Busterboy's dumpster, and goes back to sleep. In the morning he discovers a drunken bum in the living room, who proceeds to defecate on the floor. It's not, however, to his horrified disappointment, the midnight drunk. He has murdered a man.

He awaits the arrival of the police. They don't come. They never come.

"He'd become so many people," Lowell reflects,

that he no longer knew who he was anymore. . . . Locked within the same imperfect and hungover envelope of flesh were a managing editor and a guilty murderer, a man who hadn't gone home last night, a man whose marriage was on the rocks, a homeowner, a taxpayer, dupe, nice guy, and nonentity.

L. J. Davis isn't a satirist. There are no Houyhnhnms in *A Meaningful Life*. Swift is savage, but the Houyhnhnms offer a standard that one may also call an ideal. Satire has to have such an ideal, without which it is something else. Davis's novel is something else. It is a comic novel of existential loathing, written with a fine spontaneity that reflection and rewriting might have tempered— tempered the existential suggestion right out of it.

The story ends abruptly. The mansion is no longer Lowell's. Mr. Busterboy's renovation has turned it into Mr. Busterboy's idea of a house. Lowell's exertions to find meaning in a thing, object, possession haven't saved him from the emptiness and tedium of the inconsequential. The inconsequential continually threatens to drown you, to own you, to preempt your attention, till, looking up, you find yourself at the end of the night.

When I was a child living on a sugar plantation in Cuba, hardly supervised, I joined a small group of Cuban children in the evenings to hunt for the very large fireflies called *luciérnaga* in Spanish, which we would capture and keep alive in glass jars, mesh net covering their necks to let in air. Then we would venture into utterly dark fields of sugar cane, or other black corners of the Cuban night, lighting our way with our living flashlights. I think of L. J. Davis as one of those firefly-filled jars, illuminating the dark side of middle-class—and more than middle-class—efforts to find a meaningful life in what is outside of us.

THE TENDER NIGHT

JACK AND DWAYNE lived in apartment 6E in a twelve-story building facing Central Park on the Upper West Side of Manhattan. One morning in the late fifties, I moved into the apartment above theirs with my two young sons, our clothes, a few pieces of furniture, some boxes of books and games and papers, including my divorce decree, and a carton or two of kitchen odds and ends.

I met Jack a few weeks later when he rang my bell, held out a book, and inquired whether I had lost it. He had found it in the trash can at his back door, which opened onto a dimly lit, gloomy service stairway. "By accident, I guess," he added quickly, as though obliged to account for the book's presence in his trash can.

No one had claimed it yet, he said. He had checked all his neighbors. Now he was trying the tenants on my floor. If he had no luck finding the owner, he might keep the book. He loved the title, *Tender Is the Night*, although he had never heard of the writer, F. Scott Fitzgerald. I recognized my worn volume at once and took it, thanking him. It had been given to me by a friend when I was seventeen and living in a small apartment in San Francisco on Telegraph Hill.

I recall wondering how it had ended up where it had. Now and then the tenants had to use the back stairs when the elevators weren't working. It was possible that I, or the movers, had let the book fall into his can on the way up to 7E—but not likely.

There was a momentary silence during which we smiled at each other. He began to turn away then appeared to change his mind, introduced himself and held out his hand. I shook it, aware of its warmth and firmness.

I saw all of him that afternoon, as one takes in the full portrait of another person before moving in closer and noting details of face and body. Jack was in his early thirties, I guessed, boyishly handsome, tall and narrow-hipped, with short, dark brown hair. Later, after we became friends, I saw more distinctly the details of his face, its hint of secrecy, its changeability, and what I sensed was an ardent hope for affection. In the uncertainty of his smile, I felt a shock of recognition, but unlike my own smile, his was unguarded. I learned quickly that neither of us was open with others unless we felt in them the same hope—although I've made mistakes now and then.

Jack told me he'd been in the navy toward the end of World War II. I thought he must have been the picture of nauticalness in his uniform—except for that uncertainty, or perhaps it was hesitancy, in his voice and manner. He had joined the navy to avoid being drafted, he said.

I couldn't imagine him battling enemy sailors. After a few days of knowing him, I realized that he didn't want to contend with other men, but only to make love to them, sometimes to love them.

Dwayne was in a new dance company that had earned a reputation for the originality of its choreography. There were no stars yet. Dwayne would often return home to 6E exhausted from rehearsals, smoke a little marijuana, and lie down on the living-room floor to sleep for an hour or two.

Jack and I always telephoned each other before we visited, a hello and how are you. When we were together, we spoke of many things, our conversations drifting along like a slow-moving river. Our friendship deepened; even when I was tired out. I looked forward to his presence. We both seemed to brighten in each other's company.

Once, referring to a commercial kitchen cleanser, he said, "I've been told I look like Mr. Clean. But actually, I'm Mr. Dirty." He laughed as he always did at his own jokes, just as I did at mine.

One late afternoon, as I pushed open the unlocked door of his apartment, I heard a woman singing. I was so startled by the beauty of her voice, its range and muscularity, the ravishing music of her song, that I didn't move for several minutes, listening. The song ended. I entered the living room to find Jack sitting in front of his record player, watching the record still spinning. He glanced over at me, whispered, "Maria Callas singing 'Vissi d'arte' from *Tosca*."

In the hour that followed, Jack spoke about the operas he loved, and the singers, especially Maria Callas. I had studied the classical piano repertoire for a while at Juilliard but was largely ignorant of other music—except jazz. Years earlier I had overheard my mother speak scornfully about opera to one of my uncles—"all those fat people standing around bellowing at each other," she had said, and although I never consciously paid any attention to my mother's aesthetic opinions—they couldn't penetrate the obscuring darkness between us—somehow her words had been able to leave a stain for me on operatic music.

I taught in a private school that my children attended on scholarship. On two afternoons and evenings every week, I took classes at Columbia University. When I was out, I hired a sitter, usually a young Swiss woman from a nearby hostel where Swiss people stayed when they came to this country to go to school.

On a day when I reached home an hour or so before my children were due, I phoned Jack. "Should I come down or will you come up?" I asked. "Come down," he replied. "There's someone here I'd like you to meet."

Our apartments were identical: living room, dinette, narrow kitchen, two small bedrooms, a bathroom at the end of a short hallway. But the decor was dramatically different. Except the boys' bedroom, full of books and games, their discarded clothes all over the floor, the rest of my rooms looked bare, even meager. But Jack and Dwayne lived in a miniature splendor—silk drapes, elaborate candelabra on small, elegant tables, tassels on the corners of brocade pillows arranged carefully across the seat of an opulent sofa in their living room, and in one of the bedrooms, a four-poster bed with transparent white side curtains.

When Jack opened the door, four straight pins sticking out from between his lips, he led me to the spare bedroom. I saw a large woman standing there on a footstool. She was nearly covered with beige tissue paper, like a living gift being wrapped. Jack removed the pins from his mouth, explained that he was fitting her for a dress, then introduced us: "My mother, June—she's visiting the city for a few days"; me he called "a lady friend from upstairs."

She peered at me over a piece of the tissue paper that clung to one cheek and smiled as he tried to locate her waist with a tape measure. She began to talk to me at once, as though we were friends in a conversation that had been interrupted. Bits of the beige paper were caught between her lips and she spat them out moistly.

She looked like a middle-aged woman from a small Iowa town, and she was. But I had a sense of a discordance between her presentation of herself—stern, plain, straightforward, guileless—and her true nature. I noted a trace of irreverence in her comments on life—about which she said in one of her rare asides, "Well, we must put up with it . . ." I surmised she meant life in general as well as Jack's preference for men.

I tried to hold up my end of the conversation while Jack silently pinned and measured. I spoke of the pleasures of the park on the other side of the broad avenue, asked her pointless questions about the town she came from, and mentioned neighborhood crime, attributing it to poverty and hopelessness. But then she took me by surprise. "Human beings," she said, "have an inborn capacity for wickedness."

Impulsively, I told her about overhearing two Hispanic men as they walked past me on the sidewalk where I had paused for a moment. "This neighborhood is a scandal, such wickedness," one had said to the other. "It is true," the other agreed.

She laughed outright. "You see, they agree with me," she said.

Jack had spoken to me about his father's death when Jack was eleven and how he had felt a secret relief. I gathered his father had been a severe man, locked into himself with his own key. Jack's uncle, his father's only sibling, was a distinguished anthropologist at a Southern university who had gradually distanced himself from his family until they no longer even exchanged holiday cards. Jack himself had attended the University of Iowa but only for his freshman year. "I didn't find it friendly," he told me once. I wondered if there had been some murky episode to account for his having left the school.

June and I talked for a while and parted amiably enough, aware, each of us, that there was more than met the eye in the other. I returned to my apartment thinking about Jack and how he made his way in the world, making clothes or decorating apartments. His jobs were irregular. He worked occasionally for a dress designer or a store where tailoring was done. Sometimes he was employed by a decorating firm and sent on special jobs to outlying parts of the city that involved a lot of riding on subways and buses. He never complained about his long and tedious trips. He seemed to accept it all as his destiny.

Jack and I grew ever more intimate. He was fond of my children and they were fond of him. When I began to go out with Martin a few years after I had moved into the apartment house, he liked Jack, too.

What I had sensed, fleetingly, as a child with four uncles, three of whom were homosexual, had become plain as I grew older. There is as much diversity among homosexual people—in some instances, more—as there is among other people.

One autumn afternoon as I stepped down from the bus I took from work, I saw Jack walking toward me on Central Park West, his nose covered with bandages taped to his cheeks. He smiled painfully as he told me his tale. There had been a young man in the park who had encouraged Jack to follow him into a grove of trees. When they were inside it, the young man had turned quickly and hit Jack in the face, breaking his nose, then had run away laughing loudly.

Jack shrugged at my exclamation of shock. "I made a mistake that time," he said, without apparent resentment.

What he had done, and suffered as a consequence, made me shiver in a sudden awareness of the wantonness of sexual life. As I stared at his wounded face, I recognized how the wish for sensual pleasure can be accompanied by peril. Strange beasts shamble out of the self's essential solitude.

He had brief fits of anger, usually set off by the sounds of a loud radio in one of his neighbors' apartments. He would go to the neighbor's door, bang on it violently—to be heard above the din, he explained to me—and when someone opened the door to stare at him questioningly, he'd say quietly through clenched teeth, "So sorry to bother you but would you be so kind as to lower the volume on your goddamned fucking machine?" and then turn on his heel and walk away. Usually this worked, but a few tenants, insulted by his ferocity, would only turn up the volume on their radios or record players.

At some point he acquired an Airedale that he named Kelly. He seemed to love the dog with an intensity that slid easily into rage. He called it "discipline" to me, yet the blows he gave across her back taught her only fear. When I protested, he admitted he was sometimes cruel to her. He tried to excuse his actions by saying it only happened when she was too slow to obey him. I asked him if he would treat a human being so violently. He looked at me helplessly, bewildered by his own behavior.

After a few months he gave the dog away to some people he knew who lived in Bucks County, Pennsylvania, or *Pa-a-a-ah*, as he called it, drawing out the abbreviation with a grim smile as though that was the way he wished he'd addressed his father.

I visited him with less apprehension now that Kelly wasn't crouched in the living room, her muzzle resting on her paws as she watched him timidly through her thick, curly beige fur.

Dwayne traveled to other cities with the ballet company, and Jack and I spent more time together. If he had something to sew, he brought it along and sat in my living room hemming the edge of a curtain, or the skirt of a suit for a customer. Sometimes he left early when he was planning to cook something elaborate. Mostly he made simple meals for himself and Dwayne.

He told me about a lover he had had for years before Dwayne who had been a well-known television star of the period and had played a ladies' man in a weekly series. We spoke of Hollywood, where I had lived for a time, then of clothes and opera singers and music. And of life itself and its strangeness. "Do you ever have the feeling when you're walking down a street—on your way to work or whatever—that you're not yourself but a mystery guest on someone's program? And you know nothing about the way you are and you don't recognize the shoes you're wearing, or your hands, and the moment isn't a moment but somehow . . . timeless?" Jack once asked, looking up blankly as he spoke. I said, "Yes," in a voice unrecognizable to me, as though it might have issued from a chair or the open book on a table.

He told me on one of those afternoons how dreadfully his family behaved toward him—all except June, his mother—especially his professor uncle who, he said, hated him so much that when Jack's younger brother died in his childhood, his uncle had whispered to him at the funeral, "Why him? Why not you?"

One time he described a sexual moment between Dwayne and himself. Dwayne had returned home from the opening of a new ballet he was in, had stripped and lain down naked in the hall, curled up, and gone to sleep. Jack had jumped him and Dwayne, awakened, had behaved and talked like a street pickup, pretending he'd never seen Jack before and wouldn't see him again. Their late-night encounter had excluded all emotion but the driving force of desire, without mind, without heart.

Staring at my reddened face—I was not used to such confidences, even from women friends—Jack quickly said that it was "different" that time, that sexual fulfillment could be more than the sum of its bodily exertions. There was affection between the two of them, moments of tenderness.

A few months later I remarried. Martin, my children, and I moved into the A-line of the same building, into a much larger apartment on the fifth floor. A few days later when I was alone in the apartment putting away books on shelves, the bell rang and I opened the door to Jack's crumpling figure and stricken face.

"My mother—" he groaned. "She died." He wept openly like a child, without covering his face, or like someone in the first moments of shock, before grief can be dissembled. I put my arms around him. We stood in the open door, holding on to each other. June, bittersweet brave June.

Martin and I moved out of Manhattan into an apartment in Boerum Hill, Brooklyn (as reported in "Light on the Dark Side.") Jack and Dwayne were no longer lovers, although they continued to share 6E. After a month or so, Dwayne found a place of his own.

Jack had told me Dwayne was using marijuana much more as time went on, and the drug was beginning to affect his ballet career.

Jack visited us several times in Brooklyn, then moved to Melville, Long Island, where he'd found steady work in a small design firm. We didn't see each other for over a year but we spoke on the telephone. There were moments of comfortable silence in our conversations. I could visualize him sitting in a room, looking down at a little table or at the dust-free floor. He was, when it came to his surroundings, an orderly man.

Months later the firm went bankrupt. Jack moved back to New York City and I lost contact with him for over a year. By the time he turned up again, we had bought a house in a nearby neighborhood. He found our address in the telephone book and one afternoon came to visit.

He was much thinner than when I had last seen him, and for the first time since I'd known him, shabby, as shabby as a pair of rundown old shoes. He told me he'd spent months on the street—"and I mean on the sidewalks, honey," he said. He'd sheltered in doorways when he wasn't chased away by irate tenants or landlords, covering himself with pieces of cardboard and rags when the weather grew cold.

"I didn't know how mean people could be," he said. Then he laughed in his old way. "I always wanted to be a welfare queen but discovered I wasn't eligible."

But his laughter held an underlying note of hopelessness. He had been rescued, he went on, by Ben, a young accountant, who, one frigid evening, took him home to his Greenwich Village apartment. When Ben rescued him that day, what Jack possessed were a worn navy peacoat, a T-shirt, and a pair of blue jeans, in his pocket a nickel and a few pennies.

Ben seemed to love him, and after a few weeks Jack was happy again. Or so he said. I felt street life had permanently scared and scarred him. Ben had a small dog, Ninny. One afternoon when I visited the cramped small apartment, Jack bent down frequently to caress Ninny. He looked up at me suddenly. "I was really bad to Kelly," he said bleakly.

Ben came home shortly before I left. He was a small person, self-contained and unsmiling, but his eyes rested on Jack constantly, and I guessed he was devoted to him, his street prize.

When Jack told me he had AIDS, his voice held a note of insouciance as though he himself had not yet heard his own news. But I detected panic on his face, and my own heart, panicky, beat violently. I imagined him dying before me like the man who had been shot down in front of the apartment house where we had both lived years earlier.

The summer of his illness, my sons had jobs in the city and Martin and I rented a house in the countryside north of New Paltz. Jack was in a veteran's hospital on the Lower East Side of Manhattan. I visited him twice, taking the bus from New Paltz to the city and back the same day.

The AIDS wing of the hospital was neutral-looking with its pale yellow walls on which hung several inane prints. Wasted men lay like sticks in hospital beds. Jack smiled up at me as I walked toward him, and I noted how his cheeks had sunk below his cheek-bones. It was a sight that haunted me on the way home.

He had lost a lot of weight and looked as sick as he was. His face was covered with a reddish rash. As he gripped my hand, I felt his strength return momentarily, then fade, so that his fingers felt like a handful of pencils.

"A fine fix," he murmured. "Poor me. Poor Ben. He has it, too."

I nodded. I hesitated for a minute to tell him about a visit I'd had from Dwayne, but realized after my first words that Jack's former lover held only a faint interest for him now.

Dwayne had stopped by one noon at our narrow Brooklyn brownstone. When he was sitting at the kitchen table looking around restlessly, he suddenly said, "No lunch for me. Would you mind if I smoked a little pot?" I nodded. He took a hand-rolled cigarette from his jacket pocket. After half an hour, interminable to me, of a silence broken only by the sounds of his long inhalations and my own awkward words sounding grotesquely cheerful under the circumstances, Dwayne left.

Jack smiled again as he recalled his visits to our house. I had asked him to make a few things for us, curtains and the like. I was happy to see him the three or four times he came to our door. He greeted me once with, "Here I am! The gay caballero!"

I visited Jack again a few weeks later. His condition had worsened and he could barely move his head on the pillow. When he spoke, it was as if I was listening to his voice through a heavy downpour of rain.

"That book . . . ," he said. "I picked it up in the lobby of the apartment house where we met. It was on top of one of the boxes the movers brought." He ran out of breath and paused for a moment. Then he went on. "I needed a reason to meet you. I saw you smile at one of the movers. I wanted you to smile at me that way . . . *The Tender Night* . . . ," and he smiled in a ghostly way. I remembered how he had told me he loved the title.

"*Tender Is the Night*," I corrected him softly. But he had closed his eyes. I left his bedside after a few more minutes for the long trip back to the mountains.

During those hours on the bus, I stared out of the window thinking about Jack and our years of friendship, our conversations, our closeness. He was going to die. I couldn't become used to that ultimate news.

The attending nurse had our summer telephone number and she called ten days later. Jack was dead. She told me then what I found hard to bear—his body had swelled up three times its usual size, although later, in the hospital morgue, it had slowly deflated. She also told me what I was relieved to hear. Jack's uncle, the professor, had at last come through. Jack's body, at his direction, was shipped south by train and buried in a cemetery just outside of Columbia, South Carolina.

Ben outlived him by three weeks. Toward the end of that time, I telephoned the hospital where he was a patient. He picked up the phone himself. I heard his labored breathing as I identified myself. He whispered that he was glad to hear from me. He fell silent for so long that I finally, after saying his name a number of times, hung up.

FRIEDA IN TAOS

In 1935, when I was twelve, during one of the rare times my father came to see me in my grandmother's small apartment in Kew Gardens, Queens, where she and I then lived, I astonished him by quoting a few words from a poem by Witter Bynner, the title of which I've forgotten. The words were, "ready for wine? There's a cup inside."

My father had met the poet in Taxco, Mexico, he told me, when he and my mother traveled there on a brief vacation from Hollywood and the movie studio where he had worked as a screenwriter after their return from Europe the preceding year.

Bynner had been a close friend of D. H. Lawrence's, and he would amuse my parents with his lively descriptions of the frequent battles between the writer and his wife, Frieda, when plates and glasses flew through the air, hurled, he implied, with savage delight by both of them.

One evening, Bynner attended an all-night party given for Lawrence in New York City. After most of the guests had left, Bynner went to the kitchen, where he sat alone at a wooden table, feeling stale and desolate in the gray dawn. Lawrence entered the room. Seeming not to notice Bynner, he went directly to the sink, which, along with both counters, was nearly hidden by dirty dishes, took an apron from a nearby hook, tied its strings around his waist, and, whispering to himself as though reciting, began to clean up the night's excesses.

I have no idea why I memorized those few words and said them to my father. Perhaps I hoped to please him with a reference to his own heavy drinking. Perhaps not.

I had found the thin volume of Bynner's poems on one of three shelves in my grandmother's skimpy bookcase, nearly invisible among a set of *The Books of Knowledge*. I guessed it had been left there by Leopold, one of my grandmother's four sons.

Three years later I was standing before a large bookcase in the living room of a Montreal boarding school where I had been sent by Mary, my father's second wife. Behind me, two other students whispered about a third. But my attention was drawn again and again to a book, *Sons and Lovers*. I reached for it ardently, much as, I came to believe after I had read it, it had reached for me. The author was D. H. Lawrence. Many years later I read a short paragraph written by his widow, Frieda.

"His courage in facing the dark recesses of his own soul impressed me always, scared me sometimes."

The sentence was from a book written by her, *Not I but the Wind*, which my father scornfully retitled, "Not I but the Windy Old Bastard." By then I had realized how his bitterness and disappointment had deformed nearly everything in his life. *Sons and Lovers* remained for me a lighthouse of consciousness. But his mockery had recalled something to me, the story he had told me, related to him by Bynner, of Lawrence washing dishes the night of the Manhattan party. How much like Paul Morel that had been, how like his delight in helping his mother with household tasks in that novel.

Another ten years elapsed. I was half a mile from Taos, New Mexico, with Richard, whom I would marry in a few months. We had found a place to stay in the tack room of an unused stable owned by Mrs. Lois Holmes, a widow who rented cabins.

We had driven west from New York City with our cat, Edna. After a week of confinement in the car and hotels, she went wild with freedom and raced about the grounds of the Holmes property, pausing to dig shallow holes at the base of trees whose names I would learn later.

Richard had quit his job at a Manhattan public relations firm where I also worked. Our limited funds were not enough to afford a cabin. We told Mrs. Holmes that, and of our wish to spend several months in Taos. She suggested the tack room in the stable. After her husband's death several years earlier, his racehorses had been sold at auction. We took the tack room gratefully.

The stable had been painted red at one time, but the color had faded and the building had a long-forsaken look. The tack room was divided into two large spaces and two cubicles, one a toilet, the other a rudimentary kitchen with a two-burner kerosene stove, a small tin basin with one tap, and a dust-laden shelf above it that held a few rusty pots and a small frying pan.

In one of the two big rooms, a post ran lengthwise from a wall, with a saddle on it that had slipped sideways, so that at first glance it appeared as if someone had just dismounted. Worn harness straps and a bridle with a corroded bit hung from two nails that had been hammered crookedly into a narrow rafter. Spider webs, the spiders long gone, hung slackly from ceilings, in the corners where walls met, and even over the dirty glass of a big window opposite the entrance, itself a wide plank with a two-foot-square opening covered by a wire screen.

Mrs. Holmes hired two Indian men to move a few furnishings from a cabin she rarely rented. It was too close to a shed that housed three toilets and a shower room for most travelers. We made an arrangement to store food in her refrigerator.

I observed the two Indians carrying from cabin to tack room two cots, two chairs, two small tables, and lamps, along with a few plates and a handful of cutlery. There was no expression I could name on their faces, but later I concluded that it had been a kind of implacability, a resolve to endure all the abasement that came their way as though it were a triumph of a sort.

I was in my early twenties, young enough to feel the enchantment of new places. Even the metal forks and knives and spoons were thrilling to hold in my hands. Richard's divorce seemed to be taking an eternity, but divorce was a complicated process then. Our hope was to start a new life together. We both intended to write. I didn't think, beyond the next month, where we would find the money to survive. Or that there was no such thing as a new life.

Richard, born in Oklahoma, had spent his childhood and youth in New Mexico. He had gone briefly to college in Albuquerque before getting a job as a cub reporter on a local newspaper. He had wanted for years to return to New Mexico, he told me, and his long-held wish and my deep conviction about the virtue and rewards of living far from cities had carried us all the way to Taos. That first dusk we sat outside in two chairs we had brought out, holding drinks in chipped cups and watching Edna play with a bit of tumbleweed blown here and there by a fitful breeze.

The desert twilight fell like gauze over us, the stable, the cabins we glimpsed near the road. The deep quiet stilled my excitement. My thoughts had the formless drift of wind-stirred clouds in an expanse of sky, a feeling I had not experienced since childhood.

After a while, in silence, we went to the tack room. I cooked something for supper, then we washed and dried the few dishes, unpacked our portable typewriters, and went to bed.

We worked in the mornings and took long drives in the afternoons. Three or four narrow roads led out from Taos. One day we took the north road and drove into the Sangre de Cristo Mountains and found a sheep ranch where the herders were Basques from northern Spain.

I was fluent in Spanish, but I noted that two of the herders seemed reluctant to speak it, although they too were fluent. I didn't know then that the Basques had their own language, only discovering this decades later when, with ignorant familiarity, I spoke Spanish to a Basque cook employed by friends. With barely concealed offense in her voice, she said to me in a heavily accented English, "We have our own language."

We visited the ranch once more later on. The Basques were shearing the sheep. A few of the animals bleated loudly and plaintively. The large metal teeth of the shears moved in wavelike arcs, the wool fell in piles to the ground. Sometimes the shears nicked the pink flesh of a sheep, and it ran away hastily, pitiful in its nakedness. The herders laughed among themselves, but I thought I heard an underlying sympathy in their laughter. Later the wool would be washed in the large metal vats we had seen at the edge of the corral.

In the evenings we occasionally drove out to the valley a few miles east of Taos, where a gambling casino had been set up in a barn. The Taos sheriff, I noted, was in charge of the roulette wheel, and the Basque sheepherders were losing all their money at the crap table—money they had saved for months for their return to Spain, now gambled away in a desert in a far-away country.

Their melancholy stoicism about their own weakness, the ironic acceptance that underlay it, were not new to me: I had seen it in the faces of Uncle Leopold and my grandmother. I had imagined that it was only familial, but now I saw it anew, a Spanish way of responding to the self's conflicting impulses. It overcame what I had grown used to in myself—the denial of such double consciousness and a hard intention to win even as one lost. That evening in the gambling hell I wanted to touch their faces, as though in that way I might acquire some of what I imagined as the peacefulness of their resignation to their own natures.

Driving home later, Richard turned off the narrow highway onto a dirt road. In the moonlike landscape of the desert, we bumped along until we arrived at a lengthy, deep crevice. We parked and walked to its edge. Hundreds of feet below us was the Rio Grande River.

It was a brutal-looking stream of rocks and eddies and deceptively still pools of black water. In the daytime, we had waded in it. The water's force had toppled me. I went under, laughing, until fear and water stopped my mouth.

A wooden bridge built by one of the early inhabitants of Taos, John Donne, crossed the river a quarter of a mile farther on, looking, from where we stood, like a giant clothespin. I recall asking someone how his name was spelled. The answer was, just like the seventeenth-century poet's.

A few days later, I drove to a large adobe house owned by a woman who employed Indian workers to make Navajo souvenirs, including the one-toed, heavy velvet foot coverings the Pueblo Indians wore. The employer had gone to Albuquerque for the day. On a circular staircase in the entrance hall I found her daughter. She might have been fifteen, a very fat girl with a moon face from which two small eyes, dark as raisins, stared down at me. Her plump left hand gripped the railing. She had heard me arrive.

The way she stood halfway down the stairs, the fear in her face, her right hand rising suddenly to point toward the work area, didn't look convincing to me. Her voice quavered as she said, "He's drunk!"

She whispered loudly then about "his" intentions toward her, sexual, the same intentions all male Indians had toward white girls.

I didn't know what to say, so I left her there and walked to the work area. In a large room, two steps down, I found a handsome Indian youth at a workbench, very drunk indeed.

"I make you shoes," he said in a slurred voice, smiling up at me, and held up in an unsteady hand the black velvet slippers I had ordered and paid for. I thanked him and took them. When I passed the stairs, the girl was gone.

On the way home, I passed the estate of Mabel Dodge Luhan, an heiress who had established a literary colony in Taos in 1919. Tony Luhan, her husband from the Pueblo, was standing before a cluster of the hundreds of wooden birdhouses he had made for her. His back was toward me and his long black braid hung straight down like an exclamation point.

We often drove past the Taos Pueblo a few miles from the town's main square. Gaunt horses grazed in fields that adjoined the walls of the Pueblo. I sensed a multitude inside, moving about their lives. The place emitted a secret energy I hadn't detected in the facial expressions of the Indians I had seen. It was a hidden country within a country. The horses were ill-nourished—there was hardly any sustenance to be gotten from the patchy ground. Pueblo Indians kept horses, I'd been told, because they symbolized wealth and power.

One afternoon, Richard and I went to the one movie house in town. It was showing a western to a few patrons, among whom, close to the screen in the front row, sat a few Indians. When the screen filled with light, it revealed them in outline wrapped in blue or pink Sears, Roebuck blankets, as they watched Indians on horseback being chased across a prairie by yippying cowboys.

Robin, a painter from England, and his wife, Peggy, came to stay in one of Mrs. Holmes's cabins. He was visiting the United States with the intention of painting portraits of literary people and those connected with them. Inevitably, we met the couple. He told us he was working on a painting of D. H. Lawrence's widow, Frieda, who lived a few miles from Taos.

I would never have guessed she was still alive, much less that I would find myself so near to her. I recalled my father's astonishment when I quoted Witter Bynner's words to him, and I wondered if my astonishment at Robin's words were not the same as his had been at the poet's.

The painter told us that Frieda was a German baroness who had married a Nottingham literature professor, Ernest Weekly. She had had three children with him, and when she had run off with Lawrence, she had, in Robin's words, "abandoned her family."

Several days later, as I sat staring down at my typewriter, a voice asked, "Vot are you doing in dere?"

"Trying to write," I answered.

"Gut!" she said strongly, nodding at me before she disappeared from view. Later that day, Robin told me the woman was Frieda Lawrence. Of course I had already guessed it.

The next morning when I went to take a shower, I discovered a tiny snake coiled around the drain, asleep. I dressed hastily in the shirt and jeans I had just dropped on the floor and went to get Richard.

He picked up a withered tree limb from the ground, went into the shower room and killed the little snake with three blows. I noted tiny amber-colored rattles at the end of its tail. Richard said, "Its bite is as bad as the big ones."

In the afternoon I sat on a folding chair in a horse stall watching Robin set up his easel and prepare his palette. For an hour or so he used me as a practice model. As I sat there breathing in the lingering smells of horse and dung mixed with linseed oil, I dreamed of ghost horses. I sat for him again, and later on, again, and the oil sketch became a portrait.

Later that week, Robin invited us to join him and Peg for tea at Frieda's house. We drove out of Taos in their rented car. There was no traffic, the Sangre de Cristo Mountains loomed over us, the land seemed to move along with the car on low billows, and the sun bore down fiercely, a brilliant yellow dazzle that did away with the past and the future, leaving only the present. We came to two adobe ranch houses facing each other across the road. They looked as if they'd been drawn by a child.

As we drew closer, I saw an elderly woman moving clumsily about the veranda of one of the houses. An ear trumpet stuck out from beneath her Harpo Marx–like yellow hair. A graceful young man joined her, took her arm, and led her to a chair. Robin told us she was Dorothy Brett, a longtime friend of the writer's. Actually, he added, she had been Lawrence's acolyte.

I was the first up the path to Frieda's house, passing a wooden out-building halfway there. Breathlessly, I pushed open the front door and felt a soft resistance, as though pillows were piled up behind it.

But it was Frieda Lawrence's ample behind as she was bending at that same moment to open the stove door. I glimpsed burned crackers covered with melted cheese in a pan.

"At least," she said to me as she straightened up holding the pan with a kitchen towel, "Lawrence isn't here to scold me for my clumsiness with these—" and she nodded toward the cheese and crackers. She laughed then, a husky, amiable sound.

The others had caught up with me, and we followed her into the living room, where she set the pan down on a roughly carpentered table. I was startled by the large paintings that crowded the white plaster walls. "Lawrence's," she said.

I found them repellent. The subjects were naked women crawling on a stone floor, their breasts and buttocks enormous, their faces angry or as blank as balloons. The work was done in raw, brutal colors, full of energy and hysteria.

I sat down beside her on a serape-covered sofa while Richard spoke across the room with Robin and Peg. Frieda told me that a week earlier a young man from Boston had visited her to talk about Lawrence. She was hardly able to get a word in. The young man had overflowed with his worshipful paean to the novelist.

"And he had rented a horse in Albuquerque and ridden here, over seventy-five miles," she said smiling. "For the effect, you see, to get my attention to his heroic effort in the cause of Lawrence."

The burned crackers had a good taste despite their charred edges. Frieda rose at some point to fetch glasses of water. The conversation, widening like a stream, grew more general. Peg twittered away, nourishing herself, no doubt, with her own Englishness. We stayed for an hour.

As we walked silently down the slope—I was too bemused by Frieda's reality, the power of her mystery for me, to speak—I saw a short, heavy man standing in the path with his back toward us. He turned when we reached him. Robin had whispered to me that he was Angelo Ravagli, brought from Italy by Lawrence. His expression was sad, defeated. When he spoke, his Italian accent was strong, as though he'd just debarked on Ellis Island. Later I heard that he had been the model for Mellors, the gamekeeper in Lawrence's novel *Lady Chatterley's Lover*.

Robin told us more about Angelo when we were in the car. He kept a potter's wheel inside the shed, and when he wasn't gambling in the barn casino he would throw pots. I never saw one, though we visited Frieda often.

At some point, I learned that Frieda and Angelo had been denied American citizenship because they were living together illicitly. In 1950 they married, and soon after were forgiven by the government and allowed to become American citizens.

After Robin and Peg left Taos, we heard about Dorothy Brett from Frieda. She had sailed to Australia with the Lawrences, and Frieda said, "One morning on the voyage, she began to follow Lawrence into the toilet. That's when I had to put my foot down." She laughed unrestrainedly, as she was apt to do about many things.

After the first few visits to her, I guessed why she had me sit next to her always, and why she stared at me so intensely. I resembled her daughter Barbara, she said.

I wondered whether she missed her children all the time, or

only at intense moments. But Lawrence had taken up all her attention, she told us, smiling as though at someone who stood just behind us. I shivered.

Angelo was bitter, I felt, because he was lonely and wanted to live the rest of his life in his own country. He went often to the barn to gamble away Frieda's money.

It was there at the gambling hell that I learned that a rich easterner had bought an old ranch to use as a second home. It was the first time I had heard those two fateful words, "second home." It was the start of a community of second homes in New Mexico.

Richard and I frequently drove to a ranch where we would rent desert ponies for an afternoon ride. We would sit on a corral fence watching them move around, some boisterously kicking up their hind legs, most plumply calm.

After we'd chosen our mounts, we would ride into the trackless desert. Tumbleweed would blow suddenly across the sand. The wind would drop. Then it would start up again as though it had yet another word to say.

One time I caught sight of a sidewinder rattlesnake zig-zagging swiftly toward my pony. Richard had seen it at the same moment and rode to my side. These ponies, he told me, were used to snakes and knew how to dance out of their way. When I glanced back to where we had been, I saw no snake, only a corkscrew ridge in the sand.

Toward the end of our second month, I picked up our mail at the Taos post office. So far, there hadn't been much mail for us.

But today there was a long business envelope addressed to Richard. I opened it. It was from one of the heads of the agency where we had both worked in New York. I read the short paragraph.

A company vice-president had written it, saying that he hoped that Richard was enjoying his long vacation. He was looking forward to his return. There were a number of new accounts to be dealt with.

I returned to the tack room and silently held out the letter to Richard. After he had read it, I recall saying, "You told me you had quit for good." He answered no, he had always expected to return to the agency. Where had I gotten the idea that he had left it permanently? When I think back to that moment, I still feel my wretched bewilderment.

Years later, after Richard and I had been parted for many years, I went to a dinner party in Manhattan. I heard Diana Trilling, whom I had just met that evening, claim that when it came to writing about nature, Norman Mailer had it all over D. H. Lawrence.

I groaned, I imagined, quietly. But Mrs. Trilling heard me. She rose from the dinner table and marched directly out of the apartment, the door slamming behind her.

The violence of her departure was mortifying. I blushed. The poet Stanley Kunitz, sitting next to me at the table, said, "That's the second dinner party in ten days that I've seen her leave in a tantrum." I knew he wanted to comfort me. But that humiliating explosion was the occasion for Stanley to tell a Lawrence story.

Years before, he had spent a summer on the outskirts of a small French village, Vence, with a group of other young people. Stanley, along with a few others, would walk to a post office a mile or so away to collect the group's mail. One morning they passed a house on whose upper balcony sat a blanketed figure in a wheelchair, an attendant close by. Someone said, "That's D. H. Lawrence."

The next morning as they passed the house, Stanley threw a note he had written up onto the balcony. In it, he expressed his love and admiration for Lawrence's work.

The attendant reached down, picked up the note and read it to Lawrence as Stanley and the others could see and hear.

When they returned with their mail and passed the house again, Stanley glanced up at the blanketed figure on the balcony. As he did so, the figure rose to its feet and bowed toward the poet.

Several weeks later when Stanley walked by the house, the man seated in the wheelchair was no longer there.

It was 1930. D. H. Lawrence died that summer of tuberculosis. He was forty-five years old.

He had left behind brilliant work, poems, translations of Italian writers (among them novels by Giovanni Verga), essays, short stories, and the luminous "Odour of Chrysanthemums," a story that can stand, along with three of his novels—*Sons and Lovers, Women in Love,* and *The Rainbow*—among the most radiant and memorable writing of the past two hundred years.

But now his name is barely recognizable to most North American readers, and his reputation has suffered from attacks by groups who quarrel with this or that idea (some of them mad), which he always expressed with the provocation of a coal-miner's son intruding upon the English literary world. An early prudery kept *Lady Chatterley's Lover* out of print until 1959, not so very different an impulse in the government forces that would not permit American citizenship to be granted to Angelo Ravagli and Frieda Lawrence until they had married each other.

FRANCHOT TONE AT THE PARAMOUNT

FRANCHOT TONE DIED in September 1968. In 1935, when I was twelve, I saw the actor in the earliest version of the film *Mutiny on the Bounty*. I sat in a dark movie house, my knees pressed up against the unoccupied seat in front of me. Tone played one of the officers who mutinied against the cruel Captain Bligh (Charles Laughton) whom they put overboard into a small lifeboat and abandoned to the open sea.

The crew and officers returned to Tahiti. It was an exuberant story. The great ship moved through the waves, the masts creaked, the sails billowed as crew members shouted across the decks to one another amid ocean spray. Then they were in Tahiti, and Franchot Tone, wearing a sarong, a wreath of large, white-petaled blossoms hanging from around his neck, stood close to a beautiful, young Tahitian woman. Another fleshy fellow in the cast was the star of the movie, Clark Gable, a large man whose acting I found severely limited. I paid him no attention.

My knees slipped down from seatback to floor. I leaned forward, enraptured by Tone, his delicate features, his narrow-lipped mouth, the irony I thought implicit in his remote smile that assured me "I'm superior to all this play-acting . . ." and above all, by what I perceived as his nature, quixotic and spiritual.

I had been struck a great blow by the force of movie love. Later, in 1939, on spring vacation from a Montreal boarding school, I saw Tone in a Group Theatre production of *The Gentle People*.

My father, a screenwriter at the time, knew the business manager of the Group, Walter Fried, whom he called "Cousin Wally." Fried arranged for me to see the play. He smoked cigars, wore a dark fedora, and the top of his shirt was unbuttoned.

On the evening I attended the play, Cousin Wally told me through the box office grill that he had arranged for the cast to meet for drinks in a small frowzy bar across the street from the theatre. Would I like to join them there?

After the final curtain fell, I walked over to the bar, uneasy yet exalted. But Tone didn't turn up, although the rest of the cast were there. I felt a bleak relief at his absence, at the same time disappointment without end.

I had bought a dress for the occasion. "Bought" is hardly the correct word. In those days you could return clothes to stores the next day with an excuse that the dress was too tight, too loose, too anything at all. "Borrow" would be more apt.

Before Act One, I walked down the aisle to my free seat, aware of how people were staring at me. Later, in the ladies' room, I saw in a mirror that I had forgotten to remove the price tag hanging from the back of the dress. People must have noticed the large, white cardboard rectangle, size and price printed on it in big black letters. I was unembarrassed by my emotions that evening; they were all-consuming, and I was barely aware of them. But the tag shamed me. I returned the dress the next morning.

A few days later, I bought a book, *Trivia*, by an English writer, Logan Pearsall Smith, and along with a letter, sent it via Cousin Wally to Tone. As I think back now, it seems to me that Fried was highly amused by the entire incident.

I hardly recall my letter. It was probably an effort to differentiate myself from his other admirers, and to praise the book for qualities that would attest to my own sensibilities. Cousin Wally told me later that Franchot had assembled the cast and read my letter aloud to them.

Yet he answered it. Joy leapt into me when I saw the envelope. His reply was cordial, intimate, I judged. But I was faintly distressed by what I sensed was a distancing sardonic note it had. But what did I expect? Everything, I suppose.

I kept his reply in a file cabinet in the cellar of the brownstone where Martin and I now live, until a decade ago. One morning a local water main burst. A flood resulted and it took many hours for firemen to pump out the six feet of water. Tone's letter was ruined along with other correspondence and some book contracts.

When I was sixteen, I lived with an elderly alcoholic woman, a friend of my stepmother's, who had sent me to California with her.

One rainy afternoon in Hollywood, where we lived, I drove in the rain to a local drugstore to get a prescription for her. As I hastened back to where I had parked, on tiptoe to avoid the deeper puddles of water, a voice from a parked car inquired, "Where are your ballet slippers?"

It was Franchot Tone. My heart raced as I smiled in his direction but I hurried to my car through the rain which had gotten suddenly heavier.

A few years later, back in New York city, I went to see a movie of his, *Five Graves to Cairo*, I think it was titled, at the Paramount Theatre in the Broadway district. The sidewalk was crawling with adolescent girls, agitated, some crying, others laughing, as they left their places in the line to dance a few steps on the street. In that era, there were stage shows in some movie houses. The girls had all come to see and hear Frank Sinatra, a singer. The name meant nothing to me.

I found a balcony seat near three sailors who laughed raucously as they jeered at the teenagers below us in the audience, who were keening and shrieking.

A skinny young man entered the stage as a curtain was parting to reveal the orchestra behind him. He sang, holding on to the microphone, desperately I thought, as though it would save him from drowning among his worshippers. What was it that drove them crazy? Franchot Tone was, after all, a serious actor . . .

The last time I saw Tone was in a small shop on Lexington Avenue in Manhattan. The optician who owned it was an old friend, and I had joined him for a brown-bag lunch. We were sitting at the rear of the narrow store, eating sandwiches when Tone, wearing a beret, opened the door and leaned in.

In that first moment of my recognition of him, though like

me he had grown much older—I lost my breath. He smiled at me and it was such a lovely smile! All his old charm for me was in it. He asked Lou, my friend, when his eyeglasses would be ready. The optician replied but I couldn't hear language. What I felt at that moment was beyond words. My hearing returned in time to hear Tone's thanks and goodbye to Lou.

Upon first seeing him years earlier, I had been astonished by the emotions his screen presence had brought to life in me. I had loved him, in a make-believe way—the way most emotion begins—for years.

That intensity of feeling prepared me, in some fashion, for love itself, its contrarieties, its defeats, its beauty.

WAY DOWN YONDER

IN 1942, WHEN I lived in the city for many months, New Orleans was an earthly paradise for me. In 2005, it was a dreadful calamity for hundreds of thousands of people because of Hurricane Katrina and still is.

On my first morning there on an autumn day sixty-six years ago, I walked along a street bordering the French Quarter. I spotted a dusty envelope on the ground and picked it up. It was unstamped but had the address of a woman in Baton Rouge. I looked up at the wall of a city jail. The letter, I guessed, had been dropped from a slit window in a cell on a high floor. It was unsealed, and I read it:

How come you was so hard with me? I be here so long without your comfort. How come you didin bring me smokes?

Didin I ast you for them? You blame me and blame me and blame me. Im dyin here with nothin to do to pass my time.

It was written in pencil and unsigned. I carried it around with me all day then I sealed, stamped and mailed it.

On my last day in New Orleans the following spring, I went to a department store on Canal Street to buy a pair of stockings. On the first floor, between elevators, I saw two fountains next to each other. Above them, large signs read: *White* and *colored.*

In a novel I wrote that was published in 1990, *The God of Nightmares*, I included the text of the letter along with an invented incident that occurs at the drinking fountains. Separate fountains, and the letter, represent to me a large part of the life in the deep south of those days.

Since last September, 2005, I've heard two words repeated in many voices on radio and television news, *Lake Pontchartrain.*

It was on the broad steps on the western side of the lake where I occasionally sat with a writer friend, Pat, and his two nearly grown sons. The elder would gradually move away from us until he was sitting on the lowest step close to the grey-blue water that eddied faintly.

I was nineteen. I had driven across the country from California to New Orleans in a second-hand Chevrolet. I had hardly any money and needed a job and a cheap place to live. I don't recall how I found work but I did find a place to live in a former mansion on Royal Street in the French Quarter that had been converted into a rooming house. During the weeks I lived there, I always found the lower steps of the once grand stairway flooded with water. I learned, in time, that it came from a bar around the corner whose toilet had bad plumbing.

I shared a vast room with a woman who had been a member of an acting troupe in her youth. I saw her sober infrequently. She slept mostly, and when she was awake, showed me an elaborate blurred courtesy. I slept in a cot across from her large bed, and before my eyes closed at night, I would stare up at the ceiling far above with its zodiac symbols painted on a dark blue background.

From the balcony off her room, I could see two streetcars rumbling along Royal Street. One carried a sign that read. *Desire,* the other *Piety.* The nineteenth-century railing I leaned against had been designed, I believe, by the iron-maker Samuel Yellen. It was strong yet delicate like iron lace.

I found a job as a file clerk in a government office attached to a huge army installation—a hangar housing experimental war planes. Two months after I got the job, a P-59, taken aloft by a test-pilot, crashed into a meadow near the hangar. The office staff was sent home that day while a medical-technical team extracted the pilot's body and the plane parts from a crater in the ground.

The alcoholic actress became too much for me. Her former husband, a doctor, who would stop by to visit her now and then, introduced me to a couple who lived a few blocks away on St. Ann Street. I moved in with them a few days after our meeting.

Pat and Mary had both won prizes for their first novels but not much money. Mary had to continue her part-time work as a secretary. I met their friends who would visit them during evenings to sit and talk in their plain, underfurnished living room.

A narrow, two-story building, a former slaves' quarter, rose in their wild garden. It contained two rooms, a kitchen on the first floor, and on the second a small bedroom where I slept.

I loved Pat and Mary. I loved their lives, their house, their friends. In the evenings, we often drove to Canal Street in their old car where Pat parked so that he and Mary and I could observe people as they went about their lives, walking and talking peacefully or arguing, even fighting, and look at lighted store windows and cars passing us, all in an atmosphere that was purposeful yet languorous.

When I think about New Orleans, it's not only the fragrance of jasmine that I recall, not only the sound of a jazz trumpet from a Bourbon Street café, but the city itself, powerfully alive, its uniqueness manifested in every street, in the air itself. And in the French Market down by the Mississippi, a few steps from the small house on St. Ann Street.

In 1942, it was not yet "modernized." When Pat and I walked there to buy vegetables and shellfish for jambalaya (a regional dish) or something else he planned to cook that evening, the food, fresh as morning, lay in wooden barrows protected from the strong sun by awnings in vivid colors. Decades later I returned to the city for a conference, and the Market's produce lay in cement containers, and no longer suggested freshness and singularity.

When we returned home and unloaded our sacks of food, I would climb up the narrow steps to my bedroom to lie down for a few minutes. The floorboards of the room were old and didn't quite fit together, leaving broad gaps here and there. Pat and I had long conversations through these cracks while he cooked in the kitchen below.

Some afternoons when Pat wasn't at work on his second novel, he would carry an old wicker armchair to the sidewalk in front of the house to spend an hour with his black neighbor who had also brought out a chair.

Pat and Mary's house was the last residence in the white-only district. He and the neighbor spoke companionably together. They only argued when Richard Wright's novel, *Native Son*, was published during the months I spent there.

The friend who had first introduced me to Pat and Mary invited me to observe an operation at Charity Hospital. I told myself I was ready for anything. I said yes.

He introduced me to the surgeon as a "visiting intern." In the operating room, a nurse brought me a stool to stand on and a surgical mask. I watched the surgery for an hour or so as the patient's guts, released by the scalpel, floated in the air just above his belly. I pretended interest as long as I could but my bold intention to stay to the end of the operation weakened with the passing moments, and I finally asked to leave.

A few days later, the doctor drove me to a beach resort, Pass Christian, on the Gulf of Mexico. He wore a transparent bathing cap, and as we walked upon the sand, it ballooned up and down on his head. We had lunch in a hotel dining room. The waiter was a tall elderly black man who swayed on his feet as he wrote down our orders. I looked down at his shoes and saw how he had cut out holes for his wounded toes. I was very young, but I had waited on tables too. I knew a little about the suffering of waiters' feet.

One morning the three of us, Pat, Mary, and I, got into their car and set off for the Mississippi Delta. They owned a tiny two-room shack in a settlement called Boothville. The walls hummed with the buzzing of bees. The house had become, over the months, a giant honeycomb. Mary wrote and published a story about it: "The Honey House."

A few months after I returned to New York City, a painter I had frequently seen at Pat and Mary's St. Ann Street house, stopped by a small, borrowed apartment in Greenwich Village where I was staying, with news.

Pat had died the day before in Charity Hospital of a second heart attack. The painter and I stared at each other with grief-stricken faces. We didn't speak for a long time after his words: "Pat is dead."

His first heart attack, several years earlier, had come about after the publication of his prize-winning novel, *Green Margins*, about the Cajuns of the Mississippi Delta. He had made a trip—one of many over the years—to Boothville, a small Cajun community. Three men grabbed him, took him off to a patch of trees, inserted a hose into his rectum, and pumped air into him for several minutes.

He told me about this ghastly incident in a neutral voice. He understood, he said, why they had done it. They had been "shamed" by his novel, not because it contained any scandal about them, but because it made them feel exposed as a community, because they took pride in their anonymity.

He had been taken to Charity Hospital that evening. The doctors had not thought he would survive. But he did.

THE BROAD ESTATES OF DEATH

AT NOON THEY began their descent from the Organ Mountains to the valley below. The road swung from side to side, now hidden by an escarp, then flung into sight as it followed the declining slope. After a sharp turn, Harry Tilson drove the car onto a fenced shoulder and turned off the ignition. Amelia, his wife, yawned and stretched. Harry removed his jacket and folded it across the backseat. Above and behind them, the mountains baked in the midday sun.

"What's in the valley?" she asked.

"Nothing."

She picked up the map lying on the seat between them.

"When will we be there?" she asked.

"An hour or less," he answered.

"Are you scared yet? To see him?"

"I don't know. I don't think so."

He hadn't seen his father, Ben, in twenty-three years. Amelia dropped the map. "How can anyone fold these things?" she asked. The United States lay across her knees covered with the penciled record of their journey from New York City to New Mexico.

"What a long way," she murmured.

Harry stared through the open window at the pale and heat-drained land below. The visit to his father, old and sick, probably dying, had been planned as a side trip during their vacation in Taos. All morning the mountains had obscured their destination.

Until Harry glimpsed the valley, he had not expected to feel much of anything. But now, along with mounting unease, the past began to own him. It was incomprehensible, all of it. Yet he had constructed from what he recalled of his early life a comic patter for himself and his listeners. It nearly convinced him he had a place to come from, early years, all that.

The stories he told were not so comic. He didn't know why he told them. Perhaps there was something satisfying in the responses he evoked when, in the guise of regional lore, he spoke of nomadic wanderings in search of work, skeletal Fords containing all that he and his father owned, whippings administered with baling wire after his mother died giving birth to his brother, who died a few months later of some childhood disease. Sometimes in midsentence, as he remembered the traveling fairs that passed seasonally through the valley towns, recalling in the wake of their gaudy, vacuous gaiety his hope that life would be different when he was older and smarter, Harry would fall silent. But he discovered that silence had its uses too.

Now, as he gazed down at it, he was astonished to perceive the valley actually existed, and he was confronted with an almost shameful truth that he was unable to find words for. The smell of wild sage assaulted his nostrils. He closed his eyes briefly and found he was straining to catch the sound of something stirring in the silence of the mountains, just as he had when he was a child. All of it had happened. He turned on the ignition and gripped the wheel.

"Did you always live around here when you were little?" Amelia asked.

Harry put the car into second gear; the grade was steep. "Yes," he said, then, "What? I'm sorry . . ."

"I asked—"

"I know what you asked." A truck gained on them, passed, and left behind a sound of grinding gears.

"Yes, what?" she asked.

"About living here? Yes. I said yes before. When he—"

"Your father?"

"We stayed near the river. That's where the work was."

Amelia made another try at refolding the map. The ineffectual rustle of the paper irritated him.

"I had a gift for finding the cheapest cars," he said.

"When you were little?" she asked.

"I was ten. That's not little."

"Oh," she said. He sensed her disbelief. Why did she bother to question him? If he turned to look at her now he knew there would be a certain plaintive sweetness in her face.

"And then?" she asked.

"Then," he began, accelerating as the road gradually leveled off, "we packed the car and set off until we found work. He drank up the take. Saturdays, he'd end up in a saloon with a hustler and no money. I'd load them both into the car, drive them to wherever we were camped. Sometimes the lady made me breakfast—"

"—when you were ten?"

"When I was a few years older. They cried all over me," he said. His tone made her feel vaguely implicated, and she moved closer to the passenger door.

"It doesn't look as if you could get anything to grow around here," she observed somewhat stiffly.

Harry sighed and loosened his grip on the wheel. They had reached the valley floor. A few cattle stood here and there staring at the daylight, as they might have stared at darkness.

"You always think you can," Harry said. "This is a bad month. But when they irrigate—you could plant a telephone pole and it would take root."

She offered him a cigarette, and as he took it from her fingers he glanced at her and smiled briefly. Their marriage was recent, their experience of each other still fresh. Everything in the car was about them, of them—their maps and cigarettes, the suitcases in which their clothes were intermingled, a half-empty bottle of whiskey that rolled around the car floor.

He was recalling other cars, heaps of clanging, rusty parts, his father's clothes and his bundled into blankets.

She was looking at him. He was such a solitary being that she imagined him self-conceived—no parents, no past. For all his stories, she did not associate him with the complex accumulation of experience she sensed in other people.

"Look! There's a house," she said, startled, expecting only horizon and sky.

"We're almost there," he said. "Mrs. Coyle wrote the place was north of Las Cruces."

"How can people live like that?" she asked, turning her head to keep the house in view for a minute longer. It looked to her like a lump of yellow earth that had been scooped up roughly from the ground. What seemed like a doorway gave on to darkness. An inner tube rested against the dirt wall, and near it a chicken stood in a pose of expectancy. There was no other sign of life.

"It's a sod shack," he said. "You'd be surprised what you can live like."

Amelia, with their destination only minutes away, asked him a question that had bothered her since letters from Mrs. Coyle, the district nurse, and a Doctor Treviot, had arrived, telling Harry of Ben Tilson's stroke. "Will your father be crippled?" Her voice held a tremor that belied her air of detachment.

"It'll be all right," Harry said. "It's not catching. Only his right arm was affected." He had casually put his arm around her shoulder as he spoke. But he felt a sudden pain in his gut and withdrew the arm abruptly.

"What's the matter?"

"It's just that I'm getting tired of driving," he replied. He wondered why he had bothered to try and reassure her. His father could have no meaning for her, and for him Ben Tilson was a monthly check and a tax deduction. Ben was a wreck, the doctor had written. No one knew what held him together.

He knew, he thought, watching the road without seeing it,

instead seeing his father, asleep in an irrigation ditch after eigh-
teen hours of work, spring up as the water reached his bare feet, a
nightmare figure blackened with mud. It was a contemptible life for
a man. What was the use of such endurance? He despised the memory—that vision of Ben, a furious scarecrow, drunk with fatigue,
digging the irrigation ditch still deeper to receive the flow of water.

"There it is," Harry said. They had rounded a curve, and just
beyond it, oasislike, was a clump of cottonwood trees and, nailed
to the trunk of one of them, a sign that read COYLE. Harry parked a
few feet from the house. The siding and window frames were nearly
bare of paint; the window shades were drawn, and a sheet-iron roof
reflected the sunlight with brutal intensity.

For a brief moment, the two of them sat unmoving. Amelia
sensed in Harry a vast exercise of will as he reached across her
and opened the door, then got out on his side. As she stepped
to the ground, she saw a gray stoop and several scrawny chickens
roosting on its steps. A dog the color of charred wood gazed at her
blankly before resting its head back on its paws. Harry waved his
hand at the stoop, and the chickens flew lumpishly into the scrub
grass. The dog rose and wagged its skinny tail just as Mrs. Verbena
Coyle opened the screen door. She regarded them silently until a
smile widened her lips to reveal small discolored teeth. Not a hair
escaped from the thick braids wound round her head. Her pale
eyes were unblinking. The heavy contours of her face were smooth;
mass upon mass, moonlike and placid.

"I knew it was you as soon as I heard the car," she said. "Ben's
been waiting all morning—wouldn't eat his lunch. Think you might
make him eat it?"

Harry went up the steps quickly, and Amelia followed. Mrs. Coyle continued. "I tell him he's got to eat meat if he's going to get better"—she paused to extend a hand to Harry. "'I'll be on my feet soon, Verbena,' he says."

Mrs. Coyle advanced a step and held out her other hand to Amelia. "Is he any better?" Harry asked.

"He's not," Mrs. Coyle answered firmly. "There comes a time in an illness where it don't matter if you have a good day." She looked up at the sky and smacked her lips. "He's a sick man, Mr. Tilson." She released both their hands and folded her own across her stomach. "When I found him laying out in the shack, holding on to his old flatiron—he'd dug a hole right in the dirt floor with it, you know—I thought he was gone for sure. But the doctor did a lot for him. He even gets around a bit, but he's weak. That real weakness," the last words said emphatically. She nodded to Amelia. "I'm a trained nurse, you know, the only one for miles around."

"Could we see him now?" Harry asked.

"That's what you come for, isn't it?" Mrs. Coyle said. "You go round the house and I'll meet you in the back. Ben's in a little shed my husband fixed up." She entered the house.

Harry backed down the two steps and stood irresolutely, frowning down at his shoes.

"Isn't she something!" Amelia spoke in a low voice.

"Did you leave the cigarettes in the car?"

"I've got them right here," she replied quickly, holding the pack out to him. But he turned from her and set off for the back of the house. Only natural, she said to herself, inevitable.

A few cottonwood trees stood between them and the dusty

lonesome-looking two-lane road. The heat sang in the silence. The air had the texture of warmed glue.

Mrs. Coyle met them at the back door. She was accompanied by a little pale man who, as she walked, slipped in and out of sight behind her as though he were in league with her shadow.

"In there," she said and waved toward an oversize chicken coop. At her words the small man took a giant step and Mrs. Coyle looked at him with rapt amusement, then turned to them, smiling archly. "This is my husband, Gulliver Coyle," she said. Mr. Coyle grinned eerily at them and nodded. Amelia noticed how knobby his fingers were, and she recalled the dry flaked furrows they had driven past.

"Come on," Harry urged her, as though she'd held back. She felt the sting of resentment. How ridiculous he looked in his finely tailored jacket, his costly slacks, as he stood in front of the shed. The dog had slunk around the house to make a part of their group.

Mrs. Coyle, as though seized by impulse, strode up to the shed door and opened it. "They're here, Ben! Your boy's here with his wife," she cried as she stood aside to let Harry and Amelia precede her. Amelia stood back to wait for Mr. Coyle, but he shook his head no, moving his abused hands in clumsy amiability. Amelia stepped across the threshold. The room contained a bed, a rocking chair, and a tall dresser from which two middle drawers were missing. The rungs of the iron headrest were patched with white paint. An old man lay on the edge of the bed. He lifted his left hand in greeting as Amelia walked toward him. But he was looking past her, at Harry. His eyes were large, faded blue, and veined. The control apparent in the way he held his long-lipped mouth so stiffly gave way to the faintest of smiles. He barely parted his lips to speak.

"Well . . . it's been a long time," he said in a thin, grainy voice.

Harry held out a hand, which the old man touched with his fingers. "I see your hair's thinning," Ben Tilson said. He looked at Amelia then. "I lost mine young, too. Seems to run in the family." There was a moment of silence, which ended when Mrs. Coyle said with arch severity, "Will you eat your lunch now, Ben? I'll bring it in." He didn't look at her or answer, and she left the shed.

Harry sat in the rocking chair. Amelia knew he was under a strain, but still, there was no other place to sit, and she stood awkwardly in the middle of the small room until Ben pointed down at his bed with a semblance of the authority of a man who knows how to deal with women. In the space he made for her by moving a few inches very slowly, she sat down on sheets thin and gray from years of washing.

"Don't worry," Ben said. "I can move if you crowd me." She looked from father to son; a resemblance echoed back and forth between them.

"Everything going good for you?" Ben asked.

"Fairly well," Harry answered. Couldn't he give his father the satisfaction of knowing how far he had traveled away from this awful place? Harry had a fundamental frugality, she thought, a reluctance to admit obligation to anyone or anything.

"Remember your aunt Thyra?" Ben asked.

"Sure . . . of course," Harry said.

"Well, she got into trouble up in Albuquerque," Ben went on. "She kept on borrowing money, signing papers she couldn't understand."

"What did she want money for?" asked Harry irritably. "I thought you wrote last year that Winslow was doing pretty well?"

"Women get queer around a certain age, I guess. She decided she'd missed out on the grander things, bought herself one of them hairless Mexican dogs, took up smoking, bought a truckload of clothes and fifteen silk ties for Winslow. Not to leave out expensive liquor."

Harry began to laugh. Broken, sibilant, it sounded like weeping. He bent over and covered his face with his hands. When he took them away a moment later, only a faint smile remained.

They all heard Mrs. Coyle nearing the shed as she crooned to the chickens. She entered the room carrying a small tray on which a plate crowded a jelly glass of milk. "Here you are, Ben. Show your boy how you can eat!"

She put the tray on the dresser, walked between Harry and Amelia, and began to plump up the thin pillows behind Ben's head, arranging his shoulders against them with demonstrative efficiency. Ben's eyes were half-shut, but his left hand moved convulsively. His right arm was immobile on the cotton coverlet. Once the tray was on his lap, he stared up at Mrs. Coyle. With ferocity, as though the sentiment had been hoarded until this moment, he said, "I don't want this stuff!"

Mrs. Coyle, her authority questioned, was at a loss. She sighed heavily. "Well—then I'll attend to my other charges," she said, crossing to a door on the other side of the room Amelia hadn't noticed. It led to another room, into which Mrs. Coyle disappeared.

Harry asked Amelia for matches. As she began searching her bag, Mrs. Coyle reappeared, her plump hands each placed on the heads of two children who clung to her skirt.

Framed by folds of cotton were the pale protuberant foreheads and silken-skinned faces of two little girls, thick pleats of skin around their slanted eyes.

"Alice and Pearly are going to have a little walk, then their lunch, then their naps," Mrs. Coyle said in a singsong voice.

"Get this tray off'n me," Ben demanded. Harry carried the tray to the dresser as Mrs. Coyle left with the children.

"Amelia . . . you've forgotten to give me the matches," Harry said. Amelia held out a book of them as Ben's voice trembled in the close air of the room. "Verbena takes care of lots of folks around here," he said.

"I thought I'd drop in on Dr. Treviot, Dad," Harry said.

"He can't tell you nothing I don't know," Ben said. "When you're old and sick, doctors get this secret organization all rigged up. It's all about you, but you can't join it."

"No secrets," Harry said briskly. "I'll stick to the facts."

"The facts!" exclaimed Ben scornfully, just as Mrs. Coyle knocked on the door and stuck her head into the room. "Mr. Coyle is playing with the children," she announced. "Perhaps you'd come over to the kitchen, Mr. Tilson, now that I've got some time."

Amelia smiled at Ben, who didn't smile back, and followed Harry and Mrs. Coyle into the yard. Mr. Coyle was just rounding the house holding the hands of the girls. They moved torpidly beside him, their faded smocks flattened against their legs. Amelia turned from them into Mrs. Coyle's huge smile. "Perhaps you'd keep old Ben company while your husband and I talk business," she said.

Amelia cast a pleading glance at Harry; he ignored her.

She went back to the shed. The old man looked at her without much interest as she resumed her seat on the bed. "Well . . . ," he sighed.

"I've never been to this part of the country before," Amelia said. Perplexed when Ben didn't answer her right away, she fell silent.

"Harry's mother died young," he said suddenly.

"Yes. He told me."

"You were saying?"

"I've never been out here," she repeated.

"Oh?" He spoke with faint interest. Could he be falling asleep or was it that she'd lost his attention? It was as if she'd never appeared in the room. Then his voice came out of the absence in his face. His lips parted and revealed a few brown teeth.

". . . like his mother," Ben said, continuing an inner story. He went on.

"When he was little, he had fat little legs, short like this—" He placed his index finger in the dead hollow of his right arm. "No longer than my forearm. I used to run him down paths, and those fat little legs of his . . . My! He could run!" They looked at each other for a long moment. Amelia thought, it's not going to be so hard. But she felt some betrayal of Harry. Had he ever thought his father knew him in such a way?

"He always did have friends," the old man went on. "Wherever we went and stopped a bit." He looked warily at Amelia. "Maybe you didn't know that?"

"No, I didn't," she said.

"I'll be getting dressed now," he said gruffly. With his good left arm, he lifted his right onto his lap.

"Shall I go get Mrs. Coyle to help you?"

"I'll manage," he said.

She left the shed. The chickens were gathered around a pile of potato peelings. Amelia avoided them, repulsed by their scrawniness.

Harry was sitting at the kitchen table with the Coyles. Mr. Coyle was staring at his wife with doggy admiration. No one looked up as Amelia came into the kitchen.

"Your father is getting dressed," she said sharply.

Mrs. Coyle nodded. "Sure he is. He expects you to take him around the valley to visit old friends. He doesn't hardly get anywhere these days."

Harry got to his feet. "Is there anything else?" he asked.

"I've tried to tell you all of it," Mrs. Coyle replied. "There'll be no point in your seeing the doctor."

"I'd like to use your bathroom," Harry said with a touch of plaintiveness.

"Mr. Coyle will show you the facilities," Mrs. Coyle said. Her husband rose obediently, and Harry followed him out of the kitchen. The clump of their footsteps sounded very loud, as though the house were hollow. Mrs. Coyle made no effort to detain Amelia, and after a minute she walked out of the kitchen. Ben, wearing khaki pants and a faded blue work shirt, leaned against the shed door. She ran to him, but he waved her away.

"Where's the car?" he wanted to know.

Slowly, they made their way to the front of the house. He wouldn't let her take his good arm. Once they were inside the car, he seemed to ignore her. After several minutes, he reached across her and pressed the horn.

"He'll be along soon," she said.

"What's he doing in there?" Ben asked irritably. Harry emerged from the house to the sagging porch, wiping his mouth fastidiously with a handkerchief. Ben moved one foot back and forth, and Amelia felt on her cheek a drop of sweat like a tear.

"Where to?" Harry said as he got into the car.

"Toward town," Ben said.

Here and there houses like shacks rose into the yellow light of the still afternoon. Once, Amelia saw a truck without wheels, abandoned in a field. A dog ran by the side of the road, its pink tongue hanging out. They went past a porch upon which an old person sat in a rocking chair, unmoving, mouth open to the heat. As they drove by a store, Ben poked Amelia with unexpected familiarity. "You can buy a pork chop or a hoe in our store . . ." Next to it stood a gas station with a large tin bucket in front of a solitary gas tank.

"Stop here," Ben directed. Harry pulled off the road in front of what Amelia guessed was a boardinghouse. After the motor died, the two men got out of the car without a backward glance. Amelia scrambled out and followed them as they approached the steps leading up to a narrow swayed porch. In the shade of its overhang stood a cluster of old men. Their work clothes were shapeless with use and age. It crossed Amelia's mind that if touched, they'd turn to dust.

Ben neared the steps cautiously, his head down. Harry walked beside him. Amelia sensed a struggle between them as Ben edged away from his son, holding the dead arm with his other. As he placed his foot on the first of three steps, the old men began to shout his name again and again. One did a short buck-and-wing. Amelia imagined she heard the click-clack of ghostly bones.

When Ben reached the porch, he looked back triumphantly at Harry. Look what I've done, his look seemed to say; I'm somebody here in my own country.

He introduced her: "Amelia, my daughter-in-law." His voice loud. Amelia smiled, and it seemed to suffice, because the old men, Ben along with them, drifted to the other end of the porch. Amelia looked around for Harry and found him a few steps behind her. He pointed at Ben, shook his head, and sighed exaggeratedly. They listened to the loud guffaws, the moments of silence broken sharply by the rise of someone's cracked old voice, a faint mumble.

"I'll wait in the car," Amelia said. She was nearly asleep when Harry and Ben rejoined her.

That afternoon they paid another visit. All the way to the Sherman ranch, Ben was loquacious. He told stories about his friends, the ones they had just seen on the boardinghouse porch. Their stories all bore the same stamp of misfortune—long droughts, disastrous storms, grudging harvests. They had outlived it all, Ben said, they had the last laugh.

No one has the last laugh, Amelia thought.

They parked in a driveway of sorts and entered a darkened room that held a stale coolness. A rancher's huge, callused hand swept a black tomcat from a chair.

"Get off there, cat," Mr. Sherman said. "You sit right down here, Ben. It's fine to see you. So your boy come home and brought his new wife? Well now, Mrs. Tilson, why don't you go visit with Mrs. Sherman?" He pointed toward the kitchen.

Mrs. Sherman, the middle-aged woman in a housedress who

had greeted them at the front door, was making coffee. She wiped her hands on her dress and pulled out a chair at a round table for Amelia.

"You must find it different here from back East."

"Yes, it is." From the other room, she could hear the men's voices rising and falling. What could wake her up fully? Her eyes nearly closed, she looked up to see Mrs. Sherman pouring coffee into thick white mugs. She was speaking about children.

"No. We don't have any," Amelia replied listlessly to the question.

"Whatever would that be like?" exclaimed Mrs. Sherman. "My children are all grown up and they've moved away. I don't know why I bother with that cat. It spends its nights getting into fights and coming home limping with its ears unstitched. I suppose you got to have something around that's alive and don't fight with you."

"Those two children Mrs. Coyle takes care of—" Amelia began impulsively.

"Pearly's my niece's little girl. Alice comes from somewhere down the valley. Bless Verbena. It isn't everybody who would bother."

"But there are special places for children like that," Amelia insisted, remotely outraged that anyone would bless Mrs. Coyle.

"I suppose so," replied Mrs. Sherman. She put the mugs of coffee on a tray and started off to the parlor. Amelia followed, carrying a sugar bowl and a pitcher of milk. Mrs. Sherman served Ben first, placing the mug on a stool where he could reach it.

"I'm not supposed to drink coffee," Ben said. "But I will, thank you. If Verbena was here she'd knock it out of my hand." He drank the coffee slowly, only his eyes closing to show his pleasure. Amelia sat down beside Harry. He seemed unaware of her. No one spoke or moved until Ben put his emptied mug down.

"You've got to take care of yourself, Ben," Mrs. Sherman said in a kindly voice.

"Yeah . . . ," the old man sighed, opening his eyes, his mouth slack. Mr. Sherman, who had been watching him, turned his attention to Harry.

"You going back East soon?" he asked.

"This afternoon," replied Harry, shooting a warning glance at Amelia.

"It's a short visit," Mrs. Sherman remarked. Nothing more was said. And what if they were leaving? Amelia asked herself. What could be solved if they stayed longer? People went off and returned, again and again until they died. Generations of tomcats left and came back, staying home until their wounds healed. The heat was immutable.

Harry stood up and handed his mug to Mrs. Sherman. "Dad," he said. Ben looked blankly about the room. "We're going?" he asked. He too got to his feet, but this time he took Harry's arm.

"It's been grand to see you," Mrs. Sherman said. Ben nodded as though he didn't know the Shermans.

"Come again, soon," Mr. Sherman said.

Outside, the intensity of the light had diminished. As they drove back to the Coyles' house, Amelia saw far ahead the Organ Mountains, shadowed, mysterious in the twilight.

Mrs. Coyle was waiting for them on the porch. "I'm glad you brought my boy home safe," she called out amiably. Ben grunted, but whether it was from disgust or the effort of moving, Amelia couldn't guess. They walked with him to the shed, Mrs. Coyle following like fate. The sky grew plum-colored.

As soon as they went inside, Ben lay down on his bed. Mrs. Coyle covered him with a blanket and left.

"We'll be on our way," Harry said.

Ben stared up at them, his eyes empty.

"I'll keep in touch," Harry promised.

"Goodbye," Amelia said and held out her hand. He touched it with one finger. At the door, Amelia turned back. Ben hadn't moved. There was such desolation in the whole look of him, though there was no expression on his face she could name.

While Harry spoke to Mrs. Coyle, Amelia went to the car. It's over, she realized.

Harry reached into the car for his jacket, still folded across the back seat, and got in. He felt in his pockets for cigarettes and turned on the ignition at the same time. Mrs. Coyle lifted a fat white arm, the broad hand dipped, and she turned slowly and entered her house. Just as the Tilsons drove onto the road, Amelia looked back once more and saw Mr. Coyle with something between a leap and a run suddenly appear on the driveway. He too waved, then stood still, staring after them.

They drove for a while in silence.

GRACE

ONCE THEY WERE out on the street, Grace, his dog, paid no attention to John Hillman, unless she wanted to range farther than her leash permitted. She would pause and look back at him, holding up one paw instead of lunging ahead and straining against her collar as John had observed other dogs do.

On her suddenly furrowed brow, in the faint tremor of her extended paw, he thought he read an entreaty. It both touched and irritated him. He would like to have owned a dog with more spirit. Even after he had put her dish of food on the kitchen floor, she would hesitate, stare fixedly at his face until he said, heartily, "Go ahead, Grace," or, "There you are! Dinner!"

He entered Central Park in the early evening to take their usual path, and the farther he walked from the apartment house where he lived the more benign he felt. A few of the people he encountered, those without dogs of their own, paused to speculate about Grace's age or her breed.

"The classical antique dog," pronounced an elderly man in a long raincoat, the hem of which Grace sniffed at delicately.

John had decided she was about three years old, as had been estimated by the people at the animal shelter where he had found her. But most of the people who spoke to him in the park thought she looked older.

"Look at her tits. She's certainly had one litter. And some of her whiskers are white," observed a youngish woman wearing a black sweatshirt and baggy gray cotton trousers. As she looked at John her expression was solemn, her tone of voice impersonal. But he thought he detected in her words the character of a proclamation: "Tits" was a matter-of-fact word a woman could say to a man unless he was constrained by outmoded views.

What if, he speculated, inflamed by her use of the word, he had leaped upon her and grabbed her breasts, which, as she spoke, rose and fell behind her sweatshirt like actors moving behind a curtain?

"You're probably right," he said as he glanced up at a park lamp that lit as he spoke, casting its glow on discarded newspapers, fruit-juice cartons, crushed cigarette packs, and empty plastic bottles that had contained water. He had seen people, as they walked or ran for exercise, pausing to nurse at such bottles, holding them up at an angle so that the water would flow more quickly into their mouths. Perhaps they were merely overheated.

"I don't know much about dogs," he added.

She was pleasant looking in a fresh, camp-counselor style,

around his age, he surmised, and her stolid-footed stance was comradely. He would have liked to accompany her for a few minutes, a woman who spoke with such authority despite the ugliness of her running shoes. He knew people wore such cartoon footwear even to weddings and funerals these days. Meanwhile, he hoped she wouldn't suddenly start running in place or stretch her arms or do neck exercises to ease whatever stress she might be experiencing, emitting intimate groans as she did so.

When he was speaking with people, he found himself in a state of apprehension, of nervous excitement, lest he be profoundly offended by what they said or did. For nearly a year, he had dated a girl who did such neck cycles at moments he deemed inappropriate. After completing one she had done in a bar they frequented, she had asked him, "Didn't I look like a kitty-cat?" "No!" he replied, his voice acid with distaste. At once he regretted it. They spent the night lying in her bed like wooden planks. The next morning she dressed in silence, her face grim. He had tried to assuage her with boyish gaiety. She had broken her silence with one sentence: "I don't want to see you anymore."

"Have a good day," said the woman in the baggy trousers, crimping her fingers at him as she sloped down the path. He bent quickly to Grace and stroked her head. "But it's night," he muttered.

Was the interest expressed by people in the park only for his dog? Was he included in their kindly looks? When the walk was over, John felt that he was leaving a country of goodwill, that the broad avenue he would cross when he emerged from the park to reach his apartment house was the border of another country, New York City, a place he had ceased to love this last year.

Grace made for frequent difficulty at the curb. If the traffic light was green and northbound cars raced by, she sat peacefully on her haunches. But when the light changed to red and the traffic signal spelled walk, Grace balked, suddenly scratching furiously at the hardened earth at the base of a spindly tree or else turning her back to the avenue. John would jerk on the leash. Grace would yelp. It was such a high, thin, frightened yelp. John would clench his jaw and yank her across the avenue, half wishing a car would clip her.

In the elevator, a few seconds later, he would regret his loss of control. If only Grace would look up at him. But she stared straight ahead at the elevator door.

The trouble with owning a dog is that it leaves you alone with a private judgment about yourself, John thought. If a person had accused him of meanness, he could have defended himself. But with a dog—you did something cheap to it when you were sure no one was looking, and it was as though you had done it in front of a mirror.

John hoped that Grace would forget those moments at the curbside. But her long silky ears often flattened when he walked by her, and he took that as a sign. The idea that she was afraid of him was mortifying. When she cringed, or crept beneath a table, he murmured endearments to her, keeping his hands motionless. He would remind himself that he knew nothing about her past; undoubtedly, she'd been abused. But he always returned, in his thoughts, to his own culpability.

To show his good intentions, John brought her treats, stopping on his way home from work at a butcher shop to buy knucklebones. When Grace leaped up and whimpered and danced as John was opening the door, he would drop his briefcase and reach into a plastic bag to retrieve and show Grace what he had brought her. She would begin at once to gnaw the bone with the only ferocity she ever showed. John would sit down in a chair in the unlit living room, feeling at peace with himself.

After he gave her supper he would take her to the park. If all went well, the peaceful feeling lasted throughout the evening. But if Grace was pigheaded when the traffic light ordered them to walk—or worse, if the light changed when they were in the middle of the avenue and they were caught in the rush of traffic and Grace refused to move, her tail down, her rump turned under—then John, despite his resolution, would jerk on the leash, and Grace would yelp. When this happened, he had to admit to himself that he hated her.

This murderous rage led him to suspect himself the way he suspected the men who walked alone in the park, shabbily dressed and dirty, men he often glimpsed on a path or standing beneath the branch of a tree halfway up a rise. In his neighborhood there were as many muggings during the day as there were at night. Only a week earlier a man had been strangled less than one hundred yards from the park entrance. Now that it was early summer, the foliage was out, and it was harder to see the direction from which danger might come.

A day after the murder, he wondered if his cry would be loud enough to bring help. He had never had to cry out. He stood before his bathroom mirror, opened his mouth, and shut it at once, imagining he had seen a shriek about to burst forth, its imminence signaled by a faint quivering of his uvula.

Grace didn't bark—at least he'd never heard her bark—and this fact increased his worry. Would she silently observe his murder, then slink away, dragging her leash behind her?

Sometimes he wished she would run away. But how could she? He didn't let her off the leash as some owners did their dogs. Were he to do so, she was likely to feel abandoned once again.

He had got Grace because he had begun to feel lonely in the evenings and on weekends since the end of his affair with the kitty-cat girl, as he named her in memory. In his loneliness, he had begun to brood over his past. He had been slothful all his life, too impatient to think through the consequences of his actions. He had permitted his thoughts to collapse into an indeterminate tangle when he should have grappled with them.

When regret threatened to sink him, he made efforts to count his blessings. He had a passable job with an accounting firm, an affectionate older sister living in Boston with whom he spoke once a month, and a rent-controlled apartment. He still took pleasure in books. He had been a comparative-literature major in college before taking a business degree, judging that comp lit would get him nowhere. His health was good. He was only thirty-six.

Only! Would he tell himself on his next birthday that he was *only* thirty-seven, and try to comfort himself with a word that mediated between hope and dread?

He had little time to brood over the past during work, yet in the office he felt himself slipping into a numbness of spirit and body broken only by fits of the looniness he had also observed in colleagues and acquaintances. He called the phenomenon "little breakdowns in big cities."

His own little breakdowns took the form of an irritability that seemed to increase by the hour. He became aware of a thick, smothering, oily smell of hair in the packed subway trains he rode to and from work. There was so much hair, lank or curly, frizzed or straight, bushy or carved in wedges, adorned with wide-toothed combs, metal objects, bits of leather, rubber bands. There were moments when John covered his mouth and nose with one hand.

Then there was the bearded man he shared an office with. Throughout the day, with his thumb and index finger, he would coil a hair in his beard as though it were a spring he was trying to force back into his skin. When John happened to look up and catch his office-mate at it, he couldn't look away or take in a single word the man was saying.

He was in a fire of rage. Why couldn't the man keep his picking and coiling for private times?

That was the heart of it, of course: privacy. No one knew what it meant anymore. People scratched and groomed themselves, coiled their hair, shouted, played their radios at full volume, ate, even made love in public. Not that anyone called it lovemaking.

On a scrap of paper that he found on his desk, John wrote:

Name's Joe Sex
You can call me Tex
You kin have me, have me
At 34th and Lex.

He rolled it up into a ball and aimed at but missed the wastebasket. Later that day, a secretary retrieved it and read it aloud to the staff. People grew merry and flirtatious. He was thanked by everyone for cheering them up, for lightening the day.

On the weekend before he found Grace at the animal shelter, he wrote three letters to the *New York Times*. The first was to a noted psychiatrist who had reviewed a study of child development, calling it an "instant classic." John wrote: "An instant classic is an oxymoron. A classic is established over time, not in an instant."

The second was sent to a book reviewer who had described a detective story as *lovingly* written. "Lovingly," John wrote, "is not an adverb that applies to literature, especially thrillers when they concern criminal activity."

His third letter was about a term, "street smart," used by a writer to describe a novel's heroine. "This is a superficially snappy but meaningless cliché that trivializes reality," he wrote. "On the street, the truth is that people stumble about in confusion and dismay even when they are making fortunes selling illegal drugs. People are smart for only a few minutes at a time."

While he was writing the letters he felt exalted. He was battling the degradation of language and ideas. But the intoxication soon wore off. He stared down at the letters on his desk. They looked less than trivial. He crumpled them and threw them into a wastebasket.

He came to a decision then. What he needed was a living creature to take care of; an animal would be a responsibility that would anchor him in daily life.

On weekends, Grace was a boon. John played with her, wearing an old pair of leather gloves so her teeth wouldn't mark his hands. He bought rubber toys in a variety store, and she learned to chase and fetch them back to him. Once, while he lay half-asleep in his bathtub, she brought him a rubber duck. "Why Grace," he said, patting her with a wet hand, "how appropriate!"

Perhaps dogs had thoughts. How else to explain the way Grace would suddenly rise from where she was lying and go to another room? Something must have occurred to her.

She followed him about as he shaved, made breakfast, washed his socks, dusted the furniture with an old shirt. When he sat down with his newspaper, she would curl up nearby on the floor. In the three months he had owned her, she had grown glossy and sleek. He liked looking at her. Where had she come from?

As if feeling his gaze, she stared up at him. At such moments of mutual scrutiny, John felt that time had ceased. He sank into the natural world reflected in her eyes, moving toward an awareness to which he was unable to give a name.

But if he bent to pet her, she would flatten her ears. Or if he touched her when she was up, her legs would tremble with the effort to remain upright yet humble. Or so he imagined.

One day he came home from work at noon. He had felt faint while drinking coffee at his desk in the office. Grace was not at the door to welcome him. He called her. There was no response.

After a thorough search, surprised by the violent thumping of his heart, he discovered her beneath the box springs of his bed. "Oh, Grace!" he exclaimed reproachfully. As soon as he had extricated her, he held her closely, her small hard skull pressed against his throat. After a moment he put her down. "You gave me a scare," he said. Grace licked her flank. Had his emotion embarrassed her?

John's throat was feeling raw and sore, but he took Grace for a walk right away. She might have been confused by the change in her routine. At the park entrance, she sat down abruptly. He tugged at the leash. She sat on—glumly, he thought. He picked her up and walked to a patch of coarse grass and placed her on it. Dutifully, she squatted and urinated. A dozen yards or so away, John saw a black dog racing around a tree while its owner watched it, swinging a leash and smiling.

Grace seemed especially spiritless today. Later, propped up by pillows in bed and drinking tea from a mug printed with his initials—a gift from the kitty-cat girl—he wondered if Grace, too, was sick.

She was lying beneath the bedroom window, her paws

twitching, her eyes rolled back leaving white crescents below her half-closed lids. He tried to forget how he had dragged her back home after their brief outing.

Of course, animals didn't hold grudges. They forgave, or forgot, your displays of bad temper. Yet they must have some form of recollection, a residue of alarm that shaped their sense of the world around them. Grace would have been as exuberant as the black dog circling the tree if her puppyhood had been different. She pranced and cried when John came home from work, but wasn't that simply relief? My God! What did she do in the apartment all day long, her bladder tightening as the hours accumulated, hearing, without understanding, the din of the city beyond the windows?

John felt better toward dusk, after waking from a nap. He determined to take Grace to a veterinarian. He ought to have done so long ago. In the telephone directory, he found a vet listed in the west Eighties, a few blocks from his apartment house.

The next morning he called his office to say that he wouldn't be in until after lunch; he had to go to the doctor. Did the secretary sense an ambiguity in his voice when he mentioned a doctor? She didn't know that he had a dog. No one in the office knew.

Yet was it possible that his evasions, his lies, were transparent to others? And they chose not to see through them because the truth might be so much more burdensome?

He recognized that people thought him an oddball at best. His friends warned him that, at worst, he would dry up, he was so wanting in emotion. But he considered most of them to be sentimentalists, worshiping sensations that they called feelings.

"You have a transient sensation. At once you convert it into a conviction," he said to a woman sitting beside him at a dinner party. The hostess heard him, sprang to her feet, grabbed the salad bowl, with its remaining contents, and emptied it onto his head. He was dismayed, but, he managed to laugh along with the other guests, who helped to pick leaves of lettuce and strips of carrot and radish from his collar and neck.

For the rest of the evening, desolation wrapped itself around him like a mantle. Everyone, including himself, was wrong. Somehow he knew he was alive. Life was an impenetrable mystery cloaked in babble. He couldn't get the olive-oil stains out of his shirt and had to throw it out.

In the vet's waiting room, Grace sat close to John's feet, her ears rising and falling at the cries of a cat in a carrier. The cat's owner tapped the carrier with an index finger and smiled at John. "Sorry about the noise," she said. "We all get scared in the doctor's office."

She may have been right, but he shied away from her all-encompassing we. He smiled minimally and picked up a copy of *Time* magazine from a table.

When the receptionist told him to go to Room One, Grace balked. He picked her up and carried her, turning away from the cat owner's sympathetic gaze. He placed Grace on a metal examination table in the middle of a bare cubicle. A cat howled in another room.

As the doctor entered, his lab coat emanating the grim, arid smell of disinfectant, he nodded to John and looked at Grace. She had flattened herself against the table; her head was between her paws. The doctor's pink hands moved Grace's envelope of fur and skin back and forth over her bones as he murmured, "Good girl, good dog."

He took her temperature, examined her teeth, and poked at her belly. With each procedure, Grace grew more inert. "Distemper shots?" the doctor asked. John shook his head mutely. The doctor asked him more questions, but John couldn't answer most of them. Finally John explained that he'd found her in an animal shelter. The doctor frowned. "Those places weren't great even before the city cut funding for them," he said. John nodded as though in agreement, but it was all news to him. What he'd known about dogs was that they could get rabies and had to be walked at least twice a day.

The doctor said that Grace had a bit of fever. It would be best to leave her overnight for observation. John could pick her up in the morning on Saturday.

John went to his office. People remarked on his paleness and asked him what the doctor had said. "I had a fever yesterday. Probably a touch of flu," he replied. After his words they kept their distance. A secretary placed a bottle of vitamin C tablets on his desk, averting her face as she told him they were ammunition in the war against colds.

"I have leprosy," John said.

She giggled and backed away from his desk. She doesn't know what leprosy is, he guessed, or senses that it's vaguely un-American.

He kept to his section of the office the rest of the day. He was gratified that his colleagues had him pegged as a bit crazy. He had no desire to dislodge the peg. It made it easier. Thinking about that now, as he drank his third carton of tea, he didn't know what it was that was made easier.

After work, with no special reason to go home, he stopped at a bar on Columbus Avenue. He ordered a double whiskey. As he drank it, his brain seemed to rise in his skull, leaving a space that filled up with serene emptiness. He ordered a repeat, wanting to sustain the feeling, which recalled to him the moments that followed lovemaking, almost a pause of being. But as he lifted his glass, he became cautious at the thought of four whiskeys on an empty stomach, and asked a passing waiter for a steak, medium. He took his drink to a booth.

The steak, when it came, was leathery, and it reminded him of the gloves he wore when he played with Grace. At this very moment she was in a cage in the dark, bewildered but stoical. Long suffering was more like it, poor thing, carried along on the current of existence. No wonder she suddenly got up and went to another room to lie down. It wasn't thought that roused her, only a need for a small movement of freedom inside of fate. Why, after all, had he stopped in this awful, shadowy bar?

He had a few friends, most of them cocooned in partial domesticity, living with someone or seeing someone steadily. His oldest friend was married, the father of a child. Occasionally someone would introduce him to a woman in an attempt at matchmaking, feebly disguised as a dinner party.

One showed no interest in him, but another had taken him aside and asked him why he had lent himself to what was, basically, a slave auction. His impulse was to remark that no one had bid for her. Instead he asked why she had agreed to meet him. She replied that she had a sociological interest in the lifestyles of male loners in New York. He observed that life, like death, was not a style. She called him a dinosaur.

The only woman over the years for whom he had felt even a shred of interest was the mother of his friend's child. When he recognized the interest, stirred once more to life after he stopped seeing the kitty-cat girl, a sequence of scenes ran through his mind like a movie: betrayal, discovery, family disruption, himself a step-father, late child-support checks. She was steadfast and not especially drawn to him.

There had been a time when he took the kitty-cat girl out for social evenings with his friends. Their enthusiasm for her was tinged by hysteria, he noted, as though he'd been transformed from a lone wolf to a compliant sheep. Walking away from a friend's apartment where they had spent an evening, he felt like a figure in a heroic illustration: a woman-saved prodigal son.

Now he was down to a sick dog. An apartment filled with unattractive furniture awaited him. But Grace would not be there.

He was dizzy after downing such a quantity of whiskey. His fork slid from his hand to fall beneath the table. He didn't bother to search for it but continued to sit motionless in the booth, most of the steak uneaten on the plate.

It might be only the strange weakness that had come over him like a swoon, but he imagined he could feel his bodily canals drying up, his eyes dimming, the roots of his hair drying with tiny explosions like milkweed pods pressed between two fingers.

His resounding No to the kitty-cat girl, from months ago, echoed in his ears. What had prevented him from saying yes? She might have laughed and embraced him. By that magic of affection that can convert embarrassment into merriment, they might have averted all that followed. Instead she had turned away and, he thought, gone to sleep, leaving him in an agitated wakefulness in which his resentment at her fatuity kept at bay, he knew now, a harsh judgment on his own nature.

She was, after all, a very nice woman: kind, generous, full hearted. What did it matter that in bending to someone's pet or a friend's small child she assumed a high, squeaky voice, that she held her hand over her heart when she was moved, that she struck actressy poses when she showed him a new outfit or hairstyle? What had it mattered? Body to body—what did it all really matter?

He sighed and bent to retrieve the fork. In the darkness beneath the table he found a whole cigarette lying among the damp pickle-ends and crumpled napkins. *Smoke it*, he told himself as he felt the strength returning to his arms and hands. Smoking was the one thing that aroused the kitty-cat girl to anger. He'd been startled by it, so much so that he'd given up the pleasure of an infrequent cigarette after dinner in the evening. "Don't make it a religion," he'd chided her. "It's only one of a thousand things that kill people."

He summoned a waiter and asked him for a match. While he

was speaking, he heard a voice boom out, "... *and this will impact the economy.*" Someone at the bar had turned up the volume on a suspended television set. John glimpsed the speaker on the screen, an elderly man wearing steel-rimmed eyeglasses. "Impact is a noun, you stupid son of a bitch," he muttered, puffing on the cigarette.

"Always correcting my English," she had protested to him more than once. It suddenly came to him that he'd been lying to himself about how the affair had ended. He'd convinced himself that she had left his apartment, angrily, the morning after their quarrel about "kitty-cat." In fact it had taken a week, during which they met at the end of the day in his or her apartment, ate together, went to a movie, slept in bed side by side. They had not made love. When they spoke, it was of mundane matters, and when they parted in the morning, he to his office and she to the private school where she taught first grade, she had briefly pressed her cheek against his. Life has its rhythms, he told himself.

But at the end of the week, after staring down at the light supper he'd prepared, she burst out at him in words that suggested a continuation of an angry interior monologue, "—and it's not only the way I talk. You're trying to change the way I am!" She paused, then shouted, "Why don't you say anything you really mean? My God! You wouldn't acknowledge the Eiffel Tower if it fell right on you!"

He had laughed, startled at such an extravagant image. "I'd be speechless then, all right," he'd said. But he admitted he'd been clumsy.

She asked then, as she wept, how he could have said No to her so savagely. Afterward, when she was dying inside, he'd walked around the apartment with a foolish smile—as though nothing had happened between them.

She picked up her purse from the chair where she'd been sitting, not eating while he ate and kept on talking cheerfully.

"You're one big NO!" she burst out. "And you're smiling this instant . . ."

He recalled touching his face. What she'd said was true. "I don't mean to smile," he'd said. She got up and dropped her key on a kitchen counter and left the apartment.

He'd eaten her untouched supper, his mind like an empty pail. Then he'd waited for her to telephone him. He'd waited for himself to telephone her. But something had gone out of him. He had slumped into a mulelike opposition to her: she skirted life's real troubles, chirping platitudes.

He dropped the cigarette the waiter had lit for him, got to his feet, and hurried from the bar. Behind him came the waiter. John paid his bill on the sidewalk, all too aware of the stares of the public.

I will not think about her, he ordered himself as he walked home. I have cleared the decks. I'm better off.

As he unlocked the door, he called, "Grace!" Then he remembered. "Oh, Christ . . . ," he said aloud.

He took a long hot shower, emerging slack limbed and unpleasantly warm. Naked, he walked through the rooms, letting the air dry him, waving his arms, a heavy object trying to fly.

He paused before the bedroom window that looked out on Central Park. Perhaps the comradely woman out for a run, who had remarked on Grace's tits, would look up and observe to a friend, "See the cock hanging up there in that window?" But he was on the seventh floor, invisible to everything but passing birds.

He put on a ragged T-shirt and turned on the television set. As a rule he watched opera, a Friday evening news program, and now and then an old movie. Tonight he would settle for diversion. He was finding it hard to keep his mind off the way he'd left the bar without paying his check.

A news anchor was saying, "The crisis centers around . . ." He switched channels and turned up a psychologist with devilish red hair and a sharp jaw who was discussing role models and sharing. "We must share," she asserted in a tone John found menacing. "Share what!" he asked the screen. "Give me a noun or give me death. And isn't 'role model' a tautology?"

On another channel a middle-aged actress declared that after years of substance abuse—"yeah, cocaine, the whole megillah"—and loveless promiscuity, she had become a sexually mature woman, in charge of her body and her life. The male interviewer smiled and nodded without pause.

On a call-in interview, a very large Arab emir was addressed as Abdul by a caller who then asked him, "How ya doin'?" The emir's expression of stolid indifference didn't change, but he appeared to send out a glow like a hot coal.

John switched channels more quickly. In every mouth that spoke from the screen, that word, "hopefully," ownerless, modifying nothing, inserted itself amid sentences like the white synthetic packing material that protected china or glasses.

The telephone rang. Startled—no one called at this time of evening—he picked it up, and a buoyant male voice asked, "John?"

The voice was not familiar. Perhaps he'd forgotten its owner; he wasn't good with voices. "Yes," he answered. He discovered at once that it was a selling call. "Do you know me?" John asked. The voice chuckled. "Well, no, John. I don't," it replied. John hung up.

It was nearly midnight when he turned off the set and went to bed. On a nearby table lay a volume of short stories by a British writer. In one of them, the writer had stated: "You can't help having the diseases of your time."

He thought of the letters to the newspaper he'd thrown away. Why had he bothered? The apocalypse would not be brought about by debased language, would it? "I've been cracked in the head, Grace," he said to the absent dog.

His body, his brain, began a slow descent into the formless stuff of sleep. His hands fluttered at the light switch until, with what felt like his last particle of energy, he pressed it off.

At once his heart began to pound. His eyelids flew open, and he was fully awake, recalling the kitty-cat's account of her only brother's death. It had happened several months before he met her. Her brother was visiting her from the Midwest. While shaving one morning in her bathroom, he toppled over, dead from a heart attack. He had been twenty-eight.

She'd telephoned the news to their mother in Norman, Oklahoma. Their father had died of the same ailment several years earlier.

"Oh, Lord—where will we get the money to fly him home and bury him?" were her mother's first words, she'd told John.

He had expressed indignation at such petty concerns in a woman whose son had died.

"You don't understand," she had cried. "She was putting something in front of her grief—like you bar a door against a burglar. And money isn't petty when there's so little of it!"

She had been right and wrong, as he had been. But he could hardly have pursued the subject while her cheeks were covered with tears.

He turned the light back on and picked up the book of short stories, opening it at random. He read several sentences. Unable to make sense of them, he dropped the book on the table. The phone rang. He grabbed it, aware that he was breathless with hope it would be the girl. "Hello, hello?" he pleaded. A muffled voice at the other end asked, "Manuel?"

The next morning he returned to the vet's office. The waiting room was crowded with animals and their owners. Dogs panted or moved restlessly or whimpered. A brilliant-eyed cat sat on a man's lap, one of its ears nearly severed from its bloodied head.

To John's relief, the receptionist sent him at once to an examining room. The doctor was waiting for him with a grave expression on his face.

"I'm sorry to inform you that"—he turned to glance at a card lying on the table—"Grace has passed away."

John was astonished to hear himself groan aloud. The doctor gripped his arm. "Steady! Relationships with pets are deeply meaningful," he said softly. "You shouldn't blame yourself. Grace was a casebook of diseases. But it was the heartworm that finished her off."

"Heartworm!" cried John.

"It's carried by mosquitoes," the doctor replied. He relinquished John's arm.

"She didn't seem that sick," John said dully, leaning against the examining table.

"She was," the doctor stated brusquely. "And please don't lean against the table or it'll give way. Let me advise a grieving period, after which, hopefully, you'll move on. Get a new pet. Plenty of them need homes." He nodded at the door.

John held up a hand. "Wait! Had she littered?"

The doctor frowned momentarily. "Yes. I believe she had."

"What do you do with the bodies?" John asked at the door.

"We have a disposal method in place. You'll be notified," the doctor answered, taking a bottle of pink liquid from a shelf and shaking it.

On the sidewalk, John stood still, trying to compose himself. He felt a jab of pain over his navel. He loosened his belt, and the pain ceased. He had been eating stupidly of late and had certainly gained weight. He set off for his apartment.

The ceiling paint in the living room was flaking. Really he

ought to do something about it. He took a dust mop from a closet and passed it over the floor. The dust collected in feathery little piles, which he gathered up on a piece of cardboard.

Had any of Grace's puppies survived? For a few minutes, he rearranged furniture. He discovered a knucklebone beneath an upholstered chair, where Grace must have stored it. A question formed in his mind as he stooped to pick it up. Was it only her past that had made her afraid? Her puppies lost, cars bearing down on her, endless searching for food, the worm in her heart doing its deadly work. He stared at the bone, scored with her teeth marks.

As if suddenly impelled by a violent push, he went to the telephone. In a notebook written down amid book titles, opera notices, and train schedules to Boston was a list of phone numbers. He had crossed out kitty-cat's name but not her phone number. Still clutching Grace's bone, he dialed it.

On the fifth ring, she answered.

"Hello, Jean," he said.

He heard her gasp. "So. It's you," she said.

"It's me," he agreed.

"And what do you want?" She was breathing rapidly.

"I'd like to see you."

"What for?"

"Jean. I know how bad it was, the way I spoke to you."

"You were so—contemptuous!"

"I know. I had no right—"

She broke in. "No one has."

They fell silent at the same moment. Her breathing had slowed down.

"I haven't just been hanging around, you know," she said defiantly.

"I only want to speak to you."

"You want! You have to think about what other people want once a year!"

"Jean, please . . ." He dropped the bone on the table.

In a suddenly impetuous rush, she said, "It was so silly what I asked you! I'll never forget it. I can't even bear describing it to myself—what happened. All I feel is my own humiliation."

"We are born into the world and anything can happen," he said.

"What?"

"Listen. I had a dog, Grace. She got sick. Last night she died at the animal hospital. I guess I wanted to tell someone."

"I don't know what I'm supposed to do with that news," she said. "But I'm really sorry." She paused, then went on. "Poor thing," she said gently, as if speaking to someone standing beside her.

Something painful and thrilling tore at his throat. He held his breath, but still a sob burst from him. Despite its volume, he heard her say, "John? Are you all right?"

"Yes, yes . . . I don't know."

"Oh, John, I can come over this minute. I've been running, but I can change clothes in a jiffy. I don't feel you're all right."

The few tears had already dried on his cheeks. They stood in their apartments, hanging on to their telephones, trying to make up their minds if they really wanted to see each other again.

THE STOP OF TRUTH

In the Night Kitchen

ON JUNE 14, 1643, the English parliament ordered licensing of the press. All licensing authority was to be wielded by two archbishops who had the power to stop publication of any book "contrary to the Doctrine and Discipline of the Church of England."

John Milton, protesting the parliamentary order in his essay, *Areopagitica*, wrote, "(it) will be primely to the discouragement of all learning and the stop of truth, not only by exercising our abilities in what we know already, but by hindering and cropping the discovery that might be yet further made."

In Camden, New York, in the early 1970s, a mother was reading a book, *In the Night Kitchen*, by Maurice Sendak, to her seven-year old son. In the first few pages, she came upon a drawing that made her shut the book and put it aside. Subsequently she asked school officials to remove *In the Night Kitchen* from elementary school libraries.

Children, she said, were already exposed to enough profanity in the media. The school superintendent, Richard McClements, agreed with her. He did not see that the book had "sufficient merit" to be kept in libraries. Schools, he said, have "a real obligation to represent what is moral, what is honest, what is decent."

Wanda Gray, the director of elementary education in Springfield, Missouri, devised a way to mask the offense in Sendak's story. Several of the drawings in the forty copies sent to forty Springfield kindergarten classes were then altered with a black felt pen. "I think it should be covered," said she (my italics).

The it that the Camden mother and Mr. McClements appeared to have found immoral, dishonest and indecent, the it which Wanda Gray thought best to cover with what the director of curriculum development in Springfield called "shorts," was the discreetly drawn penis of a small, occasionally naked boy named Mickey.

The Springfield solution brings to mind certain religious orders which obliged their members to bathe themselves only when their bodies were entirely covered in order to avoid sexual arousal, thus, one surmises, dramatically emphasizing that which the coverings sought to conceal.

In the Night Kitchen is a dream adventure. Mickey flies through a starry night in an airplane made of bread dough to the night kitchen where three bakers—all of whom resemble Oliver Hardy—lack only milk to make morning cake. Mickey finds the milk, the cake is made, and he slides back into his bed and into dreamless sleep. As Mickey falls out of darkness into the light of the night kitchen, he loses his pajamas.

Mr. Sendak's work is always distinguished by imaginative power, wit and tenderness, and it is tenderness that is especially marked in this book, in his drawings of Mickey's infant nakedness.

Yet in the eyes of some beholders one must conclude that Mickey appears primarily as a disembodied sexual organ, and that for them, any nakedness is inherently and inarguably immoral. Most young listeners, and readers, discover their corporeality when they discover their fingers and toes, and Mickey's penis is unlikely to seem a revelation. To this writer, the intensity of the response of so many communities throughout this country reflects that strange stew of prudery and prurience which so characterizes certain aspects of American cultural life.

In Lansing, Michigan, two mothers said the book was pornographic, and opposed the use of school funds to buy books "incorporating such nudity or immorality." One of them asked, "if nudity is acceptable in a kindergarten children's story, how can I teach my children that *Playboy* is not acceptable?"

One is inclined to suggest—by *teaching* your children that *Playboy* is not acceptable.

John Milton writes: "Impunity and remissness, for certain, are the bane of a commonwealth; but here the great art lies, to discern in what the law is to bid restraint and punishment, and what things persuasion only is to work."

What I have said about Mr. Sendak's work reflects my own response to it, and the opinion of it I have arrived at. I am permitted to express this opinion by virtue of the First Amendment to the Constitution of the United States. The Amendment does not allow me to coerce others into sharing my judgment any more than it allows me to insist that all children be made to read *In the Night Kitchen*.

Wanda Gray, Mr. McClements, and the other indignant parents who found the book offensive are also permitted expression of their opinions. The First Amendment does not allow them to enforce their opinions by censorship.

"Why should we then affect a rigor contrary to the manner of God and nature," writes Milton, "by abridging or scanting those means by which books freely permitted are, both to the trial of virtue and the exercise of truth?"

In Beloit, Wisconsin, a mother of three children said, "It's our responsibility as parents to protect our children. We have all sorts of laws to protect our children, but why aren't books restricted?"

As reported in the Beloit *Daily News*, this mother promised to become more active in book selections for the schools, and to keep on looking for what she called "bad books."

From the *Areopagitica*: ". . . how shall the licensers themselves be confided in unless we confer upon them, or they assume themselves to be above all others in the land, the grace of infallibility and uncorruptedness?"

The Beloit mother also asked a question: "What right does a degree give anyone to make unchangeable rules? You don't have to have a degree to know that teaching low morals and disrespect is wrong."

In these two sentences, she manages to imply the elitism of the educated, the value of instinctive response as opposed to the hard work of informed reflection, and to reveal her own ignorance when she speaks of unchangeable rules. Rules are laws, and the most cursory knowledge of law, to the interested student, shows that it alters constantly as it reflects the contesting and changing views of the people whom it serves.

Roger Baldwin, one of the founders of the American Civil Liberties Union in 1920, was a vociferous opponent of capital punishment. A journalist asked him, "What would you feel about capital punishment if your wife was raped and murdered?"

Mr. Baldwin was quoted as replying, "In that circumstance, I would be the last person to ask."

In crises of grief and outrage, we are all the "last person to ask." It is then that we most need the principles of law to protect ourselves, and others, against our own impulses. In a less savage situation than that envisioned by the journalist who questioned Mr. Baldwin, we need the same protection against our vagaries and caprices which, when justified by ideology or by the conviction that our interpretation of religious dogma excludes all other interpretations, can lead us to level cities as well as to burn books.

Milton says, "He who destroys a good book kills reason itself, kills the image of God. . . ."

That some people regarded Mickey's nakedness in *In the Night Kitchen* as "pornographic," and "incorporating . . . immorality," and that some others even detected a subtext in Mickey's discovery of milk (i.e., nocturnal emission) did not lead to very edifying argument about the meaning of good and bad, or aesthetics. On the one side, there was rigid opposition to the book; on the other, expressions, often disdainful, of outraged democratic sensibilities.

In the best of all possible worlds, we should show respect for beliefs contrary to our own, an awareness that they are inevitable. In this democracy, we have agreed to differ.

Of course, it is a problem. Democracy is full of problems. E. M. Forster articulated its deficiency in the title of his book, *Two Cheers for Democracy*, and I believe it was Winston Churchill who declared it to be a terrible system of government but the best we have.

Books must not be censored no matter how appalling we find their content. Censorship metastasizes, moving ineluctably, often invisibly, from a part to the whole.

In *Democracy in America*, Alexis de Tocqueville wrote: "I can conceive of nothing better prepared for subjection in case of defeat than a democratic people without free institutions."

It is my belief that Mr. Sendak's book, in the long run, will continue to exist as itself, merry and intransigently human, long after the din of argument concerning Mickey's nakedness has faded away.

In any event, Mr. Sendak is in good company.

Paul IV, at a moment during his four-year papacy (1555–1559), ordered that the genitals of naked figures be covered in Michelangelo's fresco of *The Last Judgment*, in the Sistine Chapel of the Vatican. Daniele da Volterra, a contemporary painter, was given the task of covering the offending areas of the figures with underwear, or breeches. In Italian *bragha* meant breeches. Thenceforth, da Volterra was nicknamed "Il Braghettone" (the breeches maker).

Michelangelo, in a retort to the Pope concerning the nudity of the figures he had painted, said: "Tell the Pope that this is a trivial matter, and can easily be arranged. Let him straighten out the world, for pictures are quickly straightened out."

UNQUESTIONED ANSWERS

IN A CHECK-OUT line at the market, a young woman in front of me exclaimed to a companion, "Oh! It's like raining." What is it, one might wonder, that is like raining? But whatever was falling against the plate glass didn't resemble rain. It *was* rain.

Like has broken loose from hip talk, once its province, and taken root in the daily language of observation and emotion, often as involuntary as a tic. "It's like sad," said a boy of the shooting death of a classmate in a gang-beleaguered school in Brooklyn. There's a significant shade of difference between *rain* and *like rain*; between *sad* and *like sad*. Meaningless, without a grammatical function, *like* in these two sentences serves to postpone for a second or two the realization of rain and death.

To say, "It is raining"; to say, "I feel sad," is concrete. But as George Orwell wrote in 1949, the "whole tendency of modern prose is away from concreteness." To illustrate his statement, he wrote a parody of a verse from Ecclesiastes. First the verse: "I returned, and saw under the sun that the race is not with the swift, nor the battle to the strong, neither yet bread to the wise, nor yet riches to men of understanding, nor yet favor to men of skill; but time and chance happeneth to them all."

And now Orwell's modernization of it: "Objective consideration of contemporary phenomena compels the conclusion that success or failure in competitive activities exhibits no tendency to be commensurate with innate capacity, but that a considerable element of the unpredictable must invariably be taken into account."

When we hear that the youngest sibling in a family unit, encouraged by his role models, has begun to communicate interpersonally, do we gain more knowledge than if we are told that a baby has begun to talk with his mother and father?

I hope you will bear with me while I read a few scraps from a review of a book I wrote called *The Moonlight Man*. My intention is to illustrate the murder of language, and therefore of meaning, not to complain about an unsympathetic response. The reviewer writes:

> The father . . . is an alcoholic and an interesting, but fairly unproductive person . . . the daughter acts as a facilitator for his alcoholism which is not a healthy role model for students who may face this problem. The book is about her separation from her parents as individuals, but it closes with her father abandoning her. The task of final separation from parents does not belong to junior high students

and I do not think this age needs to face parental abandonment. Furthermore, if a child is dealing with an alcoholic
parent, this book does not give acceptable guidance to
work on that problem.

I believe this report to contain a basic perversion of what literature and stories are concerned with—the condition of being human.
It is written in the jargon of social science. The writer does not like
the book and is unable to say so. Instead, she evokes a contemporary vision of virtue and sin: productivity and unproductivity. The
father should be the daughter's client—or patient. The story is not
acceptable because it does not give "guidance."

What I am concerned with here is the deadening of language,
an extreme form of alienation expressed in words that have no
resonance, and absolutely no inner reference to living people. "This
age does not need to face parental abandonment," the reviewer
writes. Leaving aside the question of whether or not abandonment
is involved, what on earth is "this age"? Who need not face what?
Which boys? Which girls? What human beings?

It appears to be a tendency of some social disciplines to become
intellectually petrified and spiritually lifeless if an opposing impulse
does not come into play.

The most cursory glance at changes in thinking about human
psychology over the last fifty years suggests we can only hypothesize
about the meaning of behavior. New information is always arriving;
the last word is never in.

Partly, perhaps, because we do not have the steadying forms of
older cultures to fall back on, we are, in this country, more open

to new ideas. But we are also, it seems to me, more inclined to hail the new as absolute truth—until the next *new* comes along.

Nietzsche said, "Everything absolute leads to pathology." A physicist of our own day, Dr. David Bohm, writes that "most categories are so familiar to us that they are used almost unconsciously . . . it is possible for categories to become so fixed a part of the intellect that the mind finally becomes engaged in playing false to support them."

There is another consequence of the fossilization of intellect that is both cause and result of a dependence on categories, on everything absolute, on labels. I touched upon it in speaking of the use of *like* to postpone realization. Labels not only free us from the obligation to think creatively; they numb our sensibilities, our power to feel. During the Vietnam War, the phrase *body count* entered our vocabulary. It is an ambiguous phrase, inorganic, even faintly sporty. It distanced us from the painful reality of corpses, of dead, mutilated people.

The language of labels is like paper money, issued irresponsibly, with nothing of intrinsic value behind it, that is, with no effort of the intelligence to see, to really apprehend.

George Orwell wrote that if thought corrupts language, language can also corrupt thought. An example of that is racial expletives which, once used, eat away at the capacity of the imagination to grasp the reality of other human beings, what George Eliot described in her novel *Middlemarch* as "the deep-seated habit of direct fellow feeling with individual fellow men."

In a terrible event in Queens, New York, several years ago, white teenagers howled racial expletives as they drove one black man to his death and then savagely beat another. What is to become of us all without fellow feeling? How are we to develop it in children if we do not feel it toward them? If we treat them as a race apart, substituting management techniques and hollow classifications for the sympathy and companionship we all long for in the life we share?

Children do not have judgment; they have not lived long enough for that, or for the detachment that is part of judgment. Because of that, they need the protection of adults. But in nearly every other sense, they are simply ourselves when new.

When I was a child, people used to say, "These are the best years of your life. Just wait till you grow up!" My childhood was painful—if these were the best days, I wondered, what on earth was coming next? As I grew older, I learned that people, often born in less obviously difficult circumstances than my own, had suffered disappointment, pain, bafflement, just as I had. The years of childhood are not necessarily the best or the worst, they are the first years of our lives. When we forget that, we forget our mutual humanity, and in so doing, strip children of their dignity and mysteries.

A radio interviewer, in connection with the book of mine that I mentioned earlier, having asserted that he was an optimist, asked me why my story didn't have a more upbeat ending. People like happy endings, he said, in the vaguely threatening voice I have come to expect from optimists. "Some people don't," was all I could manage to reply. What he wanted, I felt, was untruth, a Disneyfication of story, blandness, looking on the bright side, because that is what is supposed to be good for children. He seemed indifferent to an ending that might be true to the story that preceded it.

We are not the only people in the world who like happy tragedies. From the end of the seventeenth century to 1834, *King Lear* was given a happy ending. Cordelia didn't die.

It is not fitting that children be burdened, in service to some transcendent idea of truth, with the knowledge of all the failures of human society and of individual lives, which in any case they can't assimilate. But there are so many children who have experienced those failures in their flesh and bones, in their spirits! Yet, they are creatures of hope, even in the direst circumstances—and they need hope.

"My mother groan'd! my father wept. / Into the dangerous world I leapt . . . ," wrote the poet, William Blake. Don't we sense in our very cells that it is a dangerous world? And isn't it because of that deep presentiment, that we can become brave?

I want to tell you about some of the brave children I have known.

Soon after the end of World War II, I was for a year a string reporter—the lowest rung in journalism—for an English wire service. One of the places I visited was a former vacation estate of a Prussian aristocrat in the Tatra mountains on the Polish-Czechoslovak border. The Polish government had converted it into a kind of recovery residence for children who had been born in concentration camps, or who had spent part of their childhood in them. Without exception, their parents had been murdered by the Nazis.

Our small group of reporters arrived one mid-afternoon after a lengthy, bone-chilling drive through the winter-silent landscape. It was not yet dark. There were twelve or thirteen boys and girls, and a small staff, in the grand, bleak house, its walls bare, its floors stripped of rugs and recovered with linoleum, its vast uncovered windows white with the glare from the snow-covered mountains.

It was impossible to tell the ages of the children, they were so stunted. They were very glad to see us, and they clung to us, grasping our hands as they showed us their classroom; then a former salon now filled with narrow, neatly made-up cots; a library long emptied of books, its shelves containing a few toys and games; and the dining room, where we ate an early supper with them at a long trestle table covered with yellow oilcloth.

After supper, a woman from Dublin who was among our group and who sang wonderfully, gave the children a concert. They sat with rapt attention as she sang in her sweet soprano of the Molly Maguires, of massacres and betrayals, and Irish boys with bullets in their breasts fallen on the moors.

A Yugoslav and two Czech journalists spoke Polish. The rest of us depended on an interpreter. The children wanted to know where we had come from and why, did we live in houses, and what were they like? And if we had children—where were they, with us so far away? They did not speak of their own histories except in the most indirect way, and then, not in words. They were painfully alert to any sudden movement on our part; they fell into abrupt silence in the midst of merriment when they seemed to sink into a dream, and they would suddenly burst into laughter that was almost frantic.

A boy whose English name would have been Richard asked me

through the interpreter to call him that. He didn't want his Polish name. He asked me to go with him to one of the huge gardens that surrounded the mansion. I thought he was nine or so. I was told he was fourteen.

We went through the French doors of the dining room. It was nearly dark now. He held my hand as we walked along a partly cleared path, snow-laden shrubbery leaning toward us, the bare branches of winter-blackened trees above us. It was a somber, frozen, lonely place, the heart of winter. He ran a few feet ahead of me, and with his arms and hands, brushed the snow from what I thought was a column which might have once supported some heroic or mythological statue. It was a large birdbath.

He smiled at me and pointed to the sky. He made flying motions with his arms, then fluttered his hands more and more slowly as the wings of the bird he was imitating closed around its body, and it landed on the rim of the birdbath. He turned his head at an angle, then stretched forward as though to drink. His hands fluttered once again, his arms waved, the bird flew away. He shook snow from a bush, motioned me to look closely, pointed to a twig, put his hands together beneath his chin, then gradually widened them. I kicked away some snow from the ground. The earth looked like iron. I bent down and pretended my arm was a stalk that was growing up through the soil. I opened my fingers to sniff the petals of an imaginary flower. He let out a small shout of laughter and grabbed my hand and pressed it against his head. I had understood he was describing the coming of spring.

Before we left that evening, the children sang to us. Their pale faces were flushed with the pleasure of giving us their song. When we left, they crowded around the great entrance. They wept. But they stood quietly as we backed down the cleared path to our little bus. And as we drove away, we saw them waving strongly as though to wish us a safe journey.

In the fifties, I found a job tutoring in an institution for neglected and dependent children. I will call it Sleepy Hollow. It was lodged in an old Hudson River estate thirty miles or so north of New York City. The children were black, white, and Puerto Rican. Most had been born into poverty; a few came from middle-class homes that had collapsed as a result of some of the afflictions which can turn ordinary life into a nightmare—loss of jobs, alcoholism, divorce, eruptions into daylight of long-standing incest.

Perhaps half of them had been in trouble with the law, or on the verge of it. A few had spent time in the old Bellevue Hospital in the days when shock treatment was administered nearly as commonly as aspirin. Others had been brought to the institution by a distraught family member who was either too poor to feed one more mouth, or just didn't know what to do with a wild, explosive child. The words *cope* and *handle,* and the mild delusions of grandeur they evoke, had not yet entered popular language and thought.

The children lived in cottages, where they were supposed to be supervised by married couples, mostly in their late fifties, whose main qualifications, with some exceptions, appeared to me to be a combination of stolidity and blandness. They looked as if they'd seen everything and it didn't add up to much.

Quite a few of the children, who ranged in age from eight to seventeen, attended the local elementary and high schools. I was hired to tutor those who were either too fragile or too disruptive to go off the grounds, or who could, but who were falling seriously behind in their school work.

The main house creaked with age and neglect, but from its vast windows, you could stare, if you chose, at the noble Hudson while you waited for your appointment with a worker in the social services department. The air was thickened with the characteristic smell of institutions, a sour and melancholy combination of floor wax and disinfectant. Nearly all the workers had goodwill toward their clients, and a few showed passionate concern. A psychiatrist came once a week for conferences. A minister of no particular denomination held morning services on Sunday in what had been the former owner's private chapel.

Along the banks of the Hudson, above the railroad tracks, among the trees, in spots here and there on the vast, unkempt lawns, the children gathered, living different secret lives. They appeared at meal times, did some of the chores they were supposed to do in their cottage homes, turned up one or two times out of three for their appointments with the social workers, and occasionally drifted into the chapel on Sundays. But theirs was a concealed community within the larger one of Sleepy Hollow. It was said, ruefully, in social services, that the children often did each other more good than their therapists did.

The old-timers threatened the bullies and comforted the wretched in ways that were unequivocal, often physical. They were tough; they didn't waste time or breath on tactful approaches to new members of the community who were terrorists, or else, so miserably afraid they hid under their beds.

One early evening, as I started up the steps of the old gatekeeper's lodge where my classroom was, I saw nearby a small girl weeping. I learned later that she had been brought to Sleepy Hollow that morning. Three children were gathered around her. A boy was making comical faces at her, stooping, because he was so much taller than she was, to try to make her look at him. Another boy had flung his arm around her narrow shoulders. And the third, an older girl, was holding her fingers, apparently counting them. As I drew closer I heard her say—"This little piggy went to market . . ." The little girl sobbed. The tall boy said, "Cut it out! It don't do no good. You'll use up all your water." The second boy tightened his grip on her and rocked her back and forth. She snuffled. She reached out and touched the intricate cornrows of the girl who held so tightly to the fingers of her other hand. "How do you do that?" she asked between sobs. Suddenly, like a flock of startled birds, they flew off toward a stand of larch trees, holding on to the little girl as though they could physically bear her out of her misery.

Her name was Gloria. That year, she was placed in three foster homes. Each time, she was brought back to Sleepy Hollow. She was eight, skinny and small, but the force of her rage frightened foster parents. She destroyed furniture, china, the clothes she was given, howling at the top of her lungs that she wouldn't. She wouldn't. Her refusal was monumental. She didn't want to leave the other children in the residence. In a black sea of dread, they were a secure island.

One evening, I had supper in her cottage and sat next to her.

Everyone except Gloria complained, not unreasonably, about the burnt and acrid-tasting frankfurters. The cottage parents listened placidly and imperturbably. That was their job. Gloria grinned at me and whispered, "I love these hot dogs." I think she would have eaten charcoal as long as she could stay among the children. Her trust in them since three had taken her to the larch trees and delivered her from the terror she felt, brought out her brightness and humor. She was placed, finally, in a foster home where there were many other children. That time, the placement took.

It was the aim of the administration to place as many children as possible. They didn't have much luck with boys or girls over ten.

My classroom in the gatekeeper's lodge was furnished with a splintery table, my desk, small, scarred desks for the children, a blackboard, and a single shelf holding a few battered texts on chemistry and mathematics. I was to tutor them in reading and composition. In most cases, they were far better at arithmetic than I was.

Sometimes I stayed as much as an hour beyond the prescribed time. We would tell stories then. Unlike the concentration camp children, they were eager to talk about their lives. We would also speak of animals, or ghosts or food, anything at all. They liked the high drama of revolting foods: frogs' legs, for example; sea-slugs, which I told them could be found in Chinese markets; or certain highly prized maguey worms in Mexican cuisine. At that time, rattlesnake meat had a brief, I hope, run as a delicacy in this country. Several of the children found a can of it in a grocery in one of the local towns and brought it to me one night, even remembering to bring a can opener. I failed the test gastronomically, but passed it to their satisfaction when I shrieked and pleaded with them to take the can out of my sight.

They liked to hear about my childhood in Cuba. In return, they told me appalling stories of their own early years, of beatings, of being locked in dark places, of setting fires, of tormenting animals and drunks. It was hard to listen. I soon perceived that the neutrality I had assumed was called for was not what they wanted. They needed it, perhaps, from their therapists, but not from me. I reacted pretty much as I felt. It occurred to me that what they would have liked very much was to have heard Charles Dickens read from *Oliver Twist*. It would have confirmed their sense of reality, of the truth of their own lives. It was what they knew, though it was terrible.

There are two boys I remember especially. One was twelve-year-old, illegitimate Danny, who had broken into a neighboring village liquor store one night. He was found by the police, lying among smashed bottles, dead-drunk. He was brought back to Sleepy Hollow where he lay sick and weak for several days. He was a small, thin boy with delicate Irish features. His history was told to me briefly by his social worker. His mother, an alcoholic, had become a prostitute to earn the money to maintain her drinking habit. When Danny was ten, she pushed him out onto the street and locked the door. He hung around for a week, eating out of garbage cans, sleeping in alleys, until the police picked him up. The other children told me he was "bad" to animals.

One evening he was the first to arrive at the gatehouse. He was in a temper, cursing in a way that would seem quaint in these days—a few *damns* and a *hell* or two. When I asked him what was wrong, he told me the minister had reproached him for throwing earthworms into a can of lye.

"I wanted to see what would happen," he explained without a touch of slyness. "You knew what would happen," I retorted. "You don't like what I did, either," he said. "No, I don't," I agreed.

Sensing danger, cats and stray dogs fled at Danny's approach. Someone on the staff had an idea. They got him a small donkey. He tried very hard to knock the donkey senseless. But though he punched it and kicked it, the donkey took to him and followed him faithfully. After a few weeks, he began to love it. I often saw the two of them, the donkey cropping grass, or wandering among bushes to scratch his hide, and Danny, his arm around the animal's bobbing neck, talking to it.

During my year at Sleepy Hollow, Danny, who had seemed only a large, insoluble problem, really began to get better at everything, his schoolwork, his relations with other children, and in his treatment of animals. He was witty. One evening he came to the classroom carrying one of the long bamboo poles the children were allowed to take to the banks of the river and fish. On its hook was an expiring daisy, which he had apparently plucked roots and all, from the ground. Yes, it was for me, he said in his dry little voice, adding that he wouldn't touch a flower with a ten-foot pole.

I was a smoker. He used to try to cadge cigarettes from me. Because the children liked to rummage in my handbag, I kept cigarettes in my pocket. But they had seen me smoking after class on my way to my car.

Danny stayed on one night after the children had gone. "How about giving me a couple of cigarettes?" he asked. "It's almost

Christmas." I shook my head. "Just one?" he wheedled. "Not a piece of one," I replied. "Aw—come on!" he begged. "They won't hurt me!"

My heart quickened; it was as if a remote creature had, after a silence that seemed permanent, suddenly spoken its name. What I heard inside his words was his belief that I was concerned about his well-being. I didn't give him a cigarette, but I got permission to take him for a short drive down to the river. The only thing he said was to observe with slight disdain that I didn't have a car radio. When I dropped him off, I saw the donkey emerge from the shadow of some trees and trot along after him as he went toward his cottage.

One night, there was trouble. Two older boys got into a fight in the narrow hall outside the classroom. They had gotten hold of two long barbecue forks. The phone to the main house where there was a night guard was often out of order, and it was that night. In my first moment of panic, I had tried to use it.

I grabbed the boy I knew best by his shirt collar, and holding on to it for dear life, climbed up on one of the tables. I still recall the anguish I felt. I think I said, or rather, cried out, something like, "Is this what thousands of years of human life is to come to? Is this all we are—snarling, murderous things?" This wild, vague oratory and the tears of frustration that were rolling down my cheeks, caught their attention. The fight stopped abruptly. The children stared at me with wonder and considerable amusement. The brother of the boy whose collar I had grabbed came over to me as I sank into a chair, and patted my head. "That's all right," he said soothingly, as though *I* were the child. "Don't worry. It's okay now."

What happened that night remains a mystery to me. Sometimes

I've thought the fight stopped because I said *we* instead of *you*. I'll never know.

After I left my job at Sleepy Hollow, I heard that Danny had made friends with an older boy. After lights out, they read *Huckleberry Finn* together with a flashlight. One dark night, they ran away. They made it all the way to Maryland, to the place where the Susquehanna River flows into Chesapeake Bay. They stole a rowboat. They had gotten only a few hundred yards from the shore when the owner of the boat spotted them. They were sent back to Sleepy Hollow. A long time later, when I reread *Huckleberry Finn*, I thought of Danny. I wondered if there was anyone alive who wouldn't have wanted someone to say to him, to her, "Come on up on the raft, Huck, honey. . . ."

Another of my students was Frank, the oldest boy in Sleepy Hollow. He was nearly seventeen, and he attended the local high school. He was tall and thin, quick on his feet and, as he said about himself, made for basketball. But he didn't like sports at all. What he was interested in was outer space.

He had spent most of his life in foster homes. He had a rootless quality; he always seemed at the point of departure. He perched on the edge of his desk and listened tolerantly while I tried to show him what a complete sentence was, but he was thinking of something else.

If someone had told you Frank was a sociopath, which some-one had told me, you might have had difficulty attaching that word to Frank. He loved the talking part of those evenings, after the work was done—the stories, the jokes, the drift of spoken memories.

I saw him angry once. That was when the Sleepy Hollow children who went out to schools in the neighborhood were issued special food tickets. It seemed they frequently spent the money they were allotted on candy and cigarettes, instead of lunch. The local kids did, too. Drugs were not available in those days as they are now.

Frank, and the other children, refused to go to their schools until the administration stopped the use of the tickets. It was hard enough for them to be known as institution inmates, but to be so dramatically singled out as they were at that moment when they had to hand over their maroon tickets to the cafeteria cashier was intolerable to them.

They were often bullied and baited by the local children, who exalted themselves and their own circumstances—whatever these might have really been—at the expense of the strangers in their midst, a form of cruelty not restricted to children.

When Frank was seven, he had asked his mother to take him to a movie. She said she couldn't. A friend was driving her to an appointment with a doctor. Frank told her he wished she was dead. She was killed a few hours later in an accident. Frank's father had deserted his family several years earlier. There was no one to take care of Frank and his brother. They began their foster home lives a few weeks after their mother's death.

I don't know how deeply, or in what part of his mind, he felt there to be a fatal connection between his fleeting rage, the wish that had expressed it, and the death that afternoon. I know he suffered—his very abstractedness was a form of suffering.

One night, Frank lingered on the gatehouse porch. He asked

me if I had ever worked in another place like Sleepy Hollow. I said no. Then, for some reason, I told him, as I have told you, about the concentration camp children I had met in the high Tatra mountains. I spoke a little about the Holocaust. We sat down on a step. It was a clear night, spring, with a little warmth in the air. The stars were thick.

"I never heard of anything like that," he said. He asked me what would happen to those children in the mountains. I said I didn't know, except what happens to everyone—they would have their lives, they had endured and survived the horror of the camps, and each would make what he or she could of it. He looked up at the sky.

"What's after the stars?" he asked. "What's outside of all that we're looking at?"

I named a few constellations I thought I recognized. Although his grades were low, he'd read an astronomy textbook on his own. He corrected my star guesses twice. "But what do you think about out there?" he urged.

I said there seemed to be a wall in the mind beyond which one couldn't go in imagining infinity—at least, I couldn't. "Me, neither," he said. We sat for a few more minutes, then said goodnight and walked away from the gatehouse, me to my car, and he to the cottage where he would live a few months longer before he ran away and was not heard from again by anyone in Sleepy Hollow.

The children in that residence accepted a certain amount of discipline—do your homework, make your bed, eat the carrots before the cupcake—though they complained noisily about it all. What they hated was to be told what they were. They had a heightened sensitivity to questions that weren't questions at all, but that were rooted in ironclad assumptions.

There were two or three people on the staff who were pretty sure they knew everything. They had forgotten—if they had ever known—that answers are not always synonymous with truth, which tends to fly just beyond reach in a thousand guises.

Those staff members were imprisoned in their notions as much as the children they met with weekly were imprisoned in case-history terminology. Professions require a system of reference and the language to express it, but the cost to truth is high if there is no reflection on the possibilities beyond that system. "What's outside of all we're looking at?" Frank had asked.

It is a question that appears to be inherent in our species, until we smother it with comfortable certainties. Jonathan Swift wrote that the people of Laputa were fed with "invented, simplified language," and machines were made to "educate . . . pupils by inscribing wafers, causing them to swallow it."

A protocomputer, perhaps—input, output. Can machines tell us what goes on between you and me? As the scientist Dr. Jacob Bronowski once said, a computer cannot be embarrassed or be made to feel regret. It can't feel joy. Lest we turn into machines of certainty, I think we must sustain the suspicion that there's a lot we don't know.

A decade after I left Sleepy Hollow, I was hired by a private prepatory school in New York to teach children who were failing their courses. Most of them were the offspring of alumni and were kept on in the school despite its reputation for placing accomplished students in the most exalted colleges and universities.

The G-group, as my students were called, were separated physically as well as in more subtle social ways from the rest of the student body. Our classroom was in an annex. Except for two or three, most of these children came from homes where they had their own rooms. Their closets were filled with cheerful clothes for every season. They had ice-skates, soccer balls, typewriters—but a list grows tedious. What they had was anything they wanted, or their parents thought they wanted. They were born into families which—whatever their own predilections might have been—valued learning and cultivation. Literature and music and art were as much a part of the environment as regular meals, summer camps in New England, nice clothes, and visits to pediatricians, psychiatrists and dentists when the services of such were called for.

Of course, there were children who didn't give a fig for art, music, and literature. "He won't read anything but baseball scores," a parent would tell me in tones of despair about her seventh-grader, a despair more appropriate to a death in the family than a child's reluctance to wade through *Barnaby Rudge*. These children were burdened not only with material choices; they bore from an early age their parents' fierce ambition that they aim themselves like arrows, not deviating a jot, until they had landed safely in an Ivy League college. This was in the late sixties, so as we know from the student rebellions and all their consequences, that safety was illusory.

Writing about these prep-school students, I recalled the son of an acquaintance who went to Bronx Science, a public high school with an unblemished record of graduating every senior, every year. On graduation day, my acquaintance's son was missing from the parade of seniors accepting their diplomas. He had failed and was obliged to repeat his senior year. But he was in the vicinity, outside on the sidewalk, wearing a T-shirt and jeans, shouting in jubilation and triumph, as the happy families emerged from the ceremony, "I didn't make it! I didn't make it!"

There were obviously profound differences between Gloria, Danny, and Frank, and many of the students in the New York private school. One of the most unpleasant was the privileged children's unquestioning belief that all they had was theirs by right, and that those who had less were somehow inferior. The Sleepy Hollow children hadn't the faintest idea that anything at all was owed them.

Yet, the G-group had something in common with Danny, Gloria, and Frank. They had known failure, too, in their own community. It was a paradox that these G-students were sometimes more interesting as people than their successful contemporaries in the main school. They had a certain gravity, and hardly any of the complacency that makes for endless adolescence.

One of them was a fourteen-year-old boy, Peter. He and his family had fled from Hungary during the uprising in 1956. Each family member took one small possession in their escape. Peter's was a book of Hungarian fairy tales he kept with him wherever he went. I saw it every day on his desk, the pages tattered, the cover faded. He often touched it as though it was a talisman. It was. It had been read to him in his own language, in the days before he had experienced a bitter sense of strangeness and hopelessness.

I began to have the conviction that he couldn't go on with his life unless he could give up the book. He was a lovely boy, courtly, dreamy, gentle. But although he spoke English quite well, he couldn't keep up with any of his studies. He was trying to go backward, to the days when he had been small and happy. Like Frank, he was thinking of something else.

One afternoon, I kept him after class to go over some work. The fairy tale book was there, as always, within his reach, on my desk.

"Why don't you translate one of those stories?" I asked him.

"But I can't," he exclaimed, as though I'd asked him to profane a sacred object. Perhaps I had.

"One of the short ones," I suggested. He looked through the pages of the book, many of which were clumsily repaired with tape.

"Yes," I said, not knowing quite what I meant.

"But it's better in Hungarian," he said.

"It's always better in the original," I said. "But you could try."

I would like to tell you that he took up my suggestion at once, translated the whole book, made great strides in his school work and escaped the G-group. It didn't happen that way. But he did make an effort with one of the stories, and somehow, that gave him encouragement. He was a brave child. Eventually, he got through the school and went to a small college in the Middle West. The man who was headmaster of the school during the years I taught there once said to me, "It is not unreasonable to limp in this world."

I ask these questions: What do pessimism or optimism have to do with Richard, who lived his childhood, day after day for six years, in a concentration camp? With Gloria, Danny, and Frank?

With Peter? With these living presences, immanent with human soul?

Are their lives, and ours, like sad? Like baffling? Like rapturous?

The ebbing away of religious belief has resulted in the loss of the language we need to express deep and serious feelings about our lives. How are we to give voice to despair, to exaltation and redemption?

But we can turn to great poets, great writers, to help us speak of life, of its mysteries. They, too, have reverence for the gods, and implicit in their work is the belief, as it is in religion, that everything that happens is extraordinarily important.

And so I would like to end this talk with the words of a great writer, Franz Kafka, who wrote:

"You can hold back from the suffering of the world, you have free permission to do so, and it is in accordance with your nature, but perhaps this very holding back is the one suffering you could have avoided."

OTHER PLACES

MY GRANDMOTHER AND I were obliged to live for several years in a very small apartment in a Long Island village which was, at that time, undergoing changes that would alter its village character forever, as the New York City commuting range extended further. I attended a public elementary school in the neighborhood. Every Saturday, I was allowed to go to the Inwood movie house, a mile or so from where we lived.

I don't remember the feature movies I saw there, only an inexhaustible serial called *The Invisible Man*, each of its episodes ending as the stocky actor who played the invisible man disappeared in sections, first his legs, then his arms, then his torso, until only his head remained floating above the furniture of a 1930s living room. When his head vanished, like the grin of the Cheshire Cat, it was time to go home.

If he disappeared from one place, I surmised, he must have been appearing in another. It was about that other place I mused as I walked home to the box where my grandmother and I lived, a place utterly and crushingly different from the Cuban plantation house where we had been before coming to the Long Island suburb.

I'm pretty sure I wanted to be that invisible man with his power to transfer himself where he wished simply by wrapping himself up in long lengths of some white material. I knew there was camera trickery involved, and I was not so credulous as to believe it was possible for solid flesh to be in two places at the same time. But despite that, the image on the screen held a powerful fascination for me, not dispelled by reason. I pondered it as though it were a riddle. Dimly I began to perceive that for a person to appear and disappear at will was a literal representation of something else. I began, in fact, to comprehend what an analogy was long before I had heard the word. After all, I may have said to myself, here I was walking along new sidewalks already crumbling, under limp-leafed trees, passing jerrybuilt new apartment houses in the hazy, humid summer air, yet in my mind I was running along a dirt road among fields of sugar cane under a vast tropical sky. And if that tropical landscape palled, I could go years back and find myself trudging up a long hill to a Victorian house overlooking the Hudson River on a winter day when the air crackled with cold. It was not lengths of material that made it possible to be in two places at once; it was memory.

Memory, books, and imagination. Stories took you to other places. Maxim Gorki wrote in *Childhood*, the first volume of his autobiography, that books made the world a larger place. There was a big public library in that Long Island village. Every week I came home with as many books as I could carry. And on Sundays, when most of my school friends stayed home and when the Inwood movie house was closed, I could read through the long afternoons. I could disappear from the constricted rooms of the apartment and appear in other places peopled with the stories, the imagination of writers, where a fierce convict changed the destiny of a bullied child, where a water rat and a mole picnicked on the banks of a stream, where an orphaned child led pirates to buried treasure, where a little girl drank a potion so magical she could shrink to a size that would allow her to enter an enchanted garden.

There was no television then, of course. But we did have a radio, and there were programs for children, "Mandrake the Magician," "Jack Armstrong," "The All-American Boy," "The Lone Ranger," "Fu Manchu," and many others I no longer remember. What resonating voices! What gongs, hooves of galloping horses, tooting of river boats, breaking of waves, foghorns, grinding villainous voices of rascals, clear, grand, if somewhat shallow voices of heroes and heroines, all—all invisible, yet more present, brought more to vivid life in the room where I listened than the images I see now on the television screen which occupy the space imagination once made boundless.

My grandmother told me stories, too, of her life in Spain before she was sent, at sixteen, to marry a man she had never seen. Some of her tales were comic, and some were tales of dread. My grandfather, a Spaniard from Asturias, owned a plantation far from Havana, and his young bride was plunged into a nineteenth-century colonial world that is now gone forever. It was her good fortune to come to care about this man in a marriage that had been arranged by an elderly relative of his, although like much good fortune, it didn't last very long. He died just after the end of the Spanish-American war, and her life was once again changed, violently this time, when she left the plantation, a large part of which had been burned to the ground, for the United States.

What I recall about her stories, told to me in fragments over the years I lived with her, was an underlying elegiac note, a puzzled mourning for the past. Every story, as concrete as the kitchen table where we sometimes sat, or in the living room where sunlight fell upon the floor through the rusted bars of a fire escape, had a subtext, and it is its melancholy note I now remember. Concrete stories, transcendental meanings—surface and depth.

But it was when my grandmother took me to see a play that I glimpsed the most dramatic instance of the double nature of life. She didn't speak English well, but she could read, and she must have seen a review of the play and thought it would be something I would like. We went to a Saturday matinee. The theater was small and beautiful. The play had been running on Broadway for some time. It was not a period, as I remember it, when there were special plays for children, anymore than there were special books for what we now call young adults. But because the play concerned itself with the misadventures of a high school student, many children were in the audience.

My grandmother had gotten us orchestra seats quite near the stage. I discovered that by leaning to either side I could see into the wings, see the actors prepare to leap from a waiting stillness into frantic activity on stage. But this view I caught of off-stage life seemed as dramatic to me, as much a part of theatrical illusion, as it did years later in London when, during an Old Vic production of *King Lear*, I saw a stagehand beating a huge sheet of tin to simulate the thunder on the heath.

The play was in the mode of the Andy Hardy movies of that period—a cartoon of teenage life. The hero was an inept, bumbling youth who was always being caught out in some mischief, drawing caricatures of a teacher, putting frogs in a girl's locker, failing all his courses, although in the end he triumphed over a brainy rival—intellect being considered a handicap then as it still is.

The climax of the play came when the youth got into a tangle with the school principal and was faced with expulsion. He cavorted and shrieked about the stage, making up in noise what was lacking in drama. The audience laughed and clapped at his predicament. I turned for a moment from the stage and noticed what I had not seen when my grandmother and I had sat down. In the seat next to mine was a small boy sitting next to an elderly woman in a uniform, a nurse perhaps. His legs stuck straight out, nearly touching the forestage. On each leg there was a metal brace as cruel looking as an animal trap. I knew at once, as any child would have known in those years, that he had had infantile paralysis. He was a small dark-haired boy. He had rested his chin on one clenched fist. Tears were streaming down his face.

As the school principal informed the youth sternly that he was to be expelled from school, he fell to his knees to plead for another chance, to promise he would be a model student from then on. The weeping of the small boy next to me grew more audible. I couldn't take my eyes from him. I don't recall much else about my first play. But although it has been fifty-two years since I sat in the theater, staring at that crippled child's profile, I recall his features distinctly. I remember how he tried to stifle his sobs, how he tried to cover his whole face with his hands, how the nurse put her arm around him and tried to comfort him.

I think that, where the audience saw only the antics of a clown, the little boy saw the misery of someone not only threatened with expulsion from school but expulsion from the human race—that he saw, in fact, the sadness of a person who can enter human society only as a fool because he feels no other way is open to him. Perhaps it was his illness, the shock of it, his banishment from what we choose to think of as the ordinary world of childhood, that had made him see differently, deeply, to discern suffering masked by silliness and self-caricature.

Is such deepening of consciousness only brought about by suffering? Some philosophers and many storytellers have thought so. But must we pose, against the alerted sensibilities suffering may bring, only a shallow cheerfulness? An inability or a disinclination to feel for others, even to feel for the self? Real life is too complex for such superficial oppositions. Is it conceivable that a human child does not, at some time or other, feel intimations of hardships, of conditions, of experiences far beyond the range of his or her own experience? I think not. Even in those child-rearing circumstances we have come to define as good—parental tenderness and interest, physical well-being, material comfort—is there not in any child an instinctive sense of the common vicissitudes, the afflictions, to which we are all susceptible?

I recently saw on television an ad for a children's blanket which, treated with some chemical, shines in the dark. "Make your child feel secure," said the television saleswoman cozily. Secure against what? The menace one so often detects in commercial offerings is, in some way, only a cruder form of a certain kind of psychological bullying: Be caring, sharing, loving—or else!

The paradox is that by our constant, obsessive concern with security, we imply ever more powerfully the dark forces against which security is supposed to guard us. We are afraid of the dark; the light of a chemically-treated security blanket only reveals its density. Would it not be wiser to acknowledge that our children feel, as we did when young, the uncertainties and alarms and confusion of being alive, of growing up?

The little boy with infantile paralysis had fallen right through the world of surfaces. Perhaps his grief was too great. Yet when the play was over, he clapped vigorously for the actors. I saw him struggle to his feet, smile up at his nurse, and hobble up the long aisle out of the theater. He was game. He had not been undone by his feelings for the play's poor fool. He had seen what was visible and what was invisible. I think now, looking back, that he had courage.

Recently I reread E. M. Forster's novel *A Room with a View*, and I came across a passage that struck me with great force. It was this:

> She gave up trying to understand herself, and joined the vast armies of the benighted, who follow neither the heart nor the brain, and march to their destiny by catch-words. The armies are full of pleasant and pious folk. But they have yielded to the only enemy that matters—the enemy

within. They have sinned against passion and truth, and vain will be their strife after virtue.

It is, of course, much easier in the short run, for us to fall back on catchwords when we are gripped by fear, by confusion, by intimations of the chaos which can turn our lives upside down on any sunny morning. I think of a middle-aged woman I heard about who, when she learned her father was dying, said at once that death could be a very enriching experience. Before her heart or brain could be engaged by this enormous event, she had sped away from it, staking out a claim for enrichment before death could get the drop on her.

And I think of a girl I read about in a newspaper story about young cancer patients. She had had leukemia for some months, and during the long periods of treatment for it, she was quoted as saying to her parents, "Please, please don't know everything about what is happening to me. Please don't understand my feelings too quickly."

Even in small matters we often seem too impatient to allow ourselves to be puzzled. We rush to define events, anomalies, surprises of all sorts, before we begin to know what we feel and think about them. We write off whole continents of human mysteries with inane clichés, and, sometimes, we reduce a mysterious human person, standing right in front of us, to a heap of psychological platitudes. "The eyes that fix you in a formulated phrase," wrote T. S. Eliot. And, too often, we use formulas to see by. They give off a dim light.

These formulas have come to express the only commonly held views we are supposed to share. But, as Randall Jarrell wrote in an essay, "The Taste of the Age," they have taken the place of a body of common knowledge that educated people—and many uneducated people—once had. "Fairy tales, myths, proverbs, history—the Bible and Shakespeare and Dickens, the *Odyssey* and *Gulliver's Travels*," writes Jarrell, "often things that most of an audience (now) won't understand an allusion to, a joke about." Yet, he goes on to say, "These things were the ground on which the people of the past came together."

What is integral to the works on Jarrell's list is an apprehension of the peculiar and unique situation of being human. Part of being human is, as the Spanish philosopher, Ortega y Gasset, writes, to be able to bear "that dramatic consciousness ever alive in our inmost being, and upon our feeling, like a murmuring counterpoint in our entrails, that we are only sure of insecurity."

Who was safer, I wonder, who more truly secure, at that play I saw long ago? The complacent, laughing audience who frantically applauded a mockery of adolescent suffering, or the weeping crippled child, who through his capacity to imagine, to feel, infused the play with meaning.

Children begin clear-eyed. Their vision is not clouded by sentimentality. They see the peculiarity of a thing, of a person. They see things we would rather they didn't see. They ask questions we either cannot answer or do not wish to answer. Yet we cannot bear their uncertainty and tell ourselves we must spare them it. So we hastily stop up their curiosity, their speculations, their first intimation of life's mystery with our formulas, a kind of mental spoon-feeding, about which Randall Jarrell, in the essay cited above, quotes E. M. Forster, who said: "The only thing we learn from spoon-feeding is the shape of the spoon." The contents of that spoon may change from period to period, but the impulse to shove it into a child's mouth does not seem to.

In the early years of the nineteenth century S. T. Coleridge spoke out against the formulas of his time. What he said seems to me as applicable now as it was then. He thought a good deal about writing and reading for children, and he writes in *Biographia Literaria*:

> Don't worry about the apparent terror and bloodshed in children's books, the real children's books. There is none there. It only represents the way in which little children, from generation to generation, learn in ways as painless as can be followed, the stern environment of life and death.

BY THE SEA

THE SAND CASTLE the three children had made was already top-
pling into the up-reaching tide so that, in their efforts to save it,
they would hardly have noticed the old man as he slid down the
low dune to the beach if he had not been holding a large hen
that nestled comfortably on his arm. Just behind him followed an
old woman and several young people, each of whom carried some
article, a sack of charcoal, a grill, towels, a folded canvas chair,
and so forth.

The old man set the hen down and at once it began to cluck, to
scratch and scatter the sand with a busy foolishness that delighted
the children whose castle had by then been completely washed
away. Murmuring among themselves a few yards away, the children
were hardly aware that the pleasure they were feeling at the sight
of the hen on the beach was due to the way it stayed close to the

old man as he stooped to balance a grill on a semi-circle of stones gathered by one of the young men.

This apparent attachment between hen and man which soothed the children—chilled by having spent so much time squatting in the damp sand, and who had all but forgotten their parents in their absorption in building their castle, but who were now, although unconsciously, longing to be embraced by them—made their shock all the more rending when the old man seized up the hen and wrung its neck.

The children clutched each other's cold flesh, their mouths opening in mute cries as they saw blood seep from beneath the old man's twisting hands to dye the russet feathers red. As he suddenly crouched and began to pluck away the feathers with increasing rapidity, the children, whimpering, saw advancing upon them, the sun at his back, their father whose enclosing arms they had only just been yearning for, and they recalled, as though it was from a time long gone, that he was coming to carry them out into the deep water beyond the waves—as he had always done at the end of their mornings by the sea—but now, as he drew ever nearer, he seemed to them a ravening beast.

NEWS FROM THE WORLD

NOTHING MUCH USED to happen around here. In summer there were more car accidents and fires and scandals. Dying went on year round, and in our village by the sea, most people breathed their last in the early hours of the morning. I'd heard that was so elsewhere.

There was no sound from the world in the winter. The snow and the sea closed us in. We had our own news. But in June, in the kitchens of the houses where we worked, we heard the babble of other places. In time, I learned that the people who came here expected something more than they could find in stories of soldiers burning villages far away, or of thieves stealing governments, or of the killing of politicians.

During the long evenings, we villagers went to the sea and collected the things they had thrown away or lost, bottles and change, rings and toys, and as we sifted through the sand, we found traces of their secret lives, their vices and wishes.

Last June, a vast pool of oil formed a mile from our shore. The summer people stood in groups on the edge of the sea, their faces flamed in the sunset as though they were seeing paradise.

That same June, I fell in love with an old man. I cleaned his kitchen, did his shopping, sniffed at his tubes of paint, touched his damp canvases, ironed his fine linen shirts and, each morning, straightened his scarcely rumpled bed.

When, at an early hour, he came to drink the coffee I had made him, I felt as though my eyes had fallen out of my head, and in their sockets, there was only light.

He was a thin old man, as limber as a youth. His hair was nearly white but his beard was black. His clear, pale voice flowed like a brook over a shallow bed. His slight stammer assured me he was shy despite the paintings of naked men and women that hung in the room where he painted. He spoke to me only of the weather.

"Is it a good morning?" he would ask, as though he weren't standing right in it.

"There's a mist, but it will be gone in an hour," I might say.

"A thick mist? A sea mist?" he would press.

"A ground mist," I'd reply, "just over the dunes and already lifting."

To describe him is to say nothing of what stirred me. It would be as foolish as to say the sky is blue and the sand is yellow. Words are nets through which all truth escapes.

One morning at the end of July, as I was passing by his chair, he placed his hands directly on my buttocks. I stood like a statue in the hollow center of which an animal flutters and scrabbles frantically to escape. When I got home that day, my children looked like strangers, and my husband's name tasted in my mouth like metal.

All through August, while I cleaned his little house behind the dunes, we spoke of mist, fog, wind, heat and rain. But when he rested his hands on various parts of my body, I waited in silence until he went back to his coffee. During those moments, I burned with a flame that was both hot and cold.

When I thought of the winter months, when the old man would be gone, the little house shuttered against the freezing wind, I knew what it would be like to feel death creeping around my feet.

I began to read the newspapers from the city which you could only buy in my village during the three months of summer, but what I read was weak and sickly. It had not the power to turn me from this terrible love that had struck me down and crushed me in my fortieth year. I longed only to submit to the torment of that light which filled my head those mornings. I watched him walk toward me with his youth's light step across the rag rug of the parlor.

"Good morning," we each said, and it was as though my heart burst loose from its nest of blood and flew like a bird toward the sky.

All summer, the pool of oil had moved closer and closer to the shore. Men came in boats and tried to bait it as though it was a wild beast. There were always fires on the beach at night, and around them people sang and embraced, their faces turned away from the dark sea.

"Will you accompany me to the shore?" the old man asked me one noon, just as I had tucked my apron away in a paper sack.

We sat on the sand among the crowd who called out to each other as they pulled thick, oily strands of devil's apron from the water.

We sat, each with our arms around our knees; our shoulders touched. Mixed with the smell of salt was his own fragrance, linseed oil and laundered linen, and the green pine soap I bought for him at the store.

Dying birds lay around our feet, and an arm's length away was a sand shark whose jaw opened and slowly stiffened.

He rose to his feet so lightly, I thought he had only sighed. Before I could cry out, he was waist high in the oil and water, flinging seabirds out upon the beach, while all around people laughed and clapped their hands.

I reached him as he fell. I carried him through the crowd whose faces had gone cold and angry.

I undressed him in the kitchen. In the narrow tub that stood on claw feet, I bathed him in warm water. I washed the oil from the wings of his hair and rinsed away every drop of it from the most tender and private parts of his body. Then I dressed him in fresh clothes I had ironed myself, and I tied the laces of his shoes and combed his damp beard.

In the kitchen, I fed him whiskey and coffee. At last the color came back to his cheeks.

He wanted me, he said, to leave the village and my children and my husband, to return with him to the city he came from. He said that there, each night, we would hear music in a different place.

I listened to him for an hour, hearing parts of his voice I'd not heard before. While he spoke, he often gripped his fine old hands together as though he were pressing something out of himself. He said there was no future for me in the village.

"You live on the edge of things," he said.

When he had finished, he lay back against the chair, his eyelids fluttering. I stood up. I folded my apron and said I wouldn't go with him although I loved him better than my village or his city or anything that walked or flew or crawled.

This winter I have often gone to look at the house where he lived. It is blowing away, a board here, a shingle there.

Inside the scarf which I wrap around my throat and jaw, I can taste my own moist breath. Inside the sleeves of my coat, where I've drawn them against the cold, my hands form cups to hold the balls of his feet, the joints of his kneecaps, the small cheeks of his behind, the angel's wings of his narrow shoulder blades.

No one will come back this summer to his house or any other house. Our beach is black with oil. Our birds are dead or gone. The fish lie frozen beneath the ooze. The dune grass cannot grow. Officials come every week and note down what news they can find in the tides of black muck. They speak only among themselves in the dunes, the wind pressing their coat collars against their clean-shaven jaws.

It is too late for reports. We are starving here in our village. At last, we are at the center.

SITTING DOWN AND ALONE

BEVERLY TINKER HANDED the letter to her husband as he came through the door of their apartment on Riverside Drive in New York City. He took it eagerly, sure it was from their son, Daniel, in his senior year at the University of Wisconsin.

"It's not from Danny," she said. "It's your Boston friend." He thought she sounded derisive. In the near darkness of the small foyer, she stood unmoving, blocking his way to the living room.

"Are we to receive letters from Daniel only?" he asked.

"I didn't say that."

Gerald hung his coat on a wire hanger and pushed it into the coat-crowded hall closet. Then turning to her, he asked, "What's the matter? Does it strike you as odd—an old friend writing to me?"

"Old friend—you haven't seen him since you were twelve."

"Next time I'm in Boston, I'll call up a girl I knew when I was twelve."

"Fine."

He leaned against the closet door and stared at her.

"Fine," he repeated. "Just fine. Why are you behaving like I called up a woman instead of aging Jack Crowder?"

She suddenly clasped her hands. "I don't understand why you can't go to a movie or read a book when you go on these trips," she said. "It's the picture of you I have—sitting on the edge of a hotel bed, *idly* dialing the phone because you've *idly* recalled someone from your past. But you've always been that way. Walking the streets all night rather than spend even three minutes just sitting down, alone."

"I haven't *always* been any way. If you'd been with me, I wouldn't have even thought of calling Jack."

"That's exactly what I mean!"

"He wasn't in! All I did was leave a message I'd called."

"What has that got to do with it?"

"I'm going out!" he shouted, opening the closet door and dragging his coat from the hanger.

"Where?" she asked. She bent to turn on a small lamp on the foyer table.

"To find that old gang of mine," he replied angrily. They fell silent. He stood there holding his coat, thinking how burdensome they could be to each other sometimes—just burdens, nothing else.

"What's the matter?" he asked in a subdued voice. "You didn't even say hello to me."

"I'm sorry," she replied. "Hello."

He hung his coat up again. Then he held out the letter to her.

"No. I don't want to read it," she said. Her anger had gone, and he knew she wouldn't take the letter now because she was mortified by her own behavior.

After dinner, Gerald set his portable typewriter on the coffee table in the living room and opened Jack's letter. The small distinct handwriting struck him as somewhat inhuman. He picked up the first sheet.

"Dear Gerald," it began. "When I have finished my day's work I grow aware of a painful silence. I begin to listen to my own small noises. I cap my pen, shut a drawer, drop a paper clip which I don't trouble to find, move an ashtray or two. I've done the reading, gone over notes, marked papers. I pick up a journal, hoping to find some item that might have escaped me the first time around. I chew my eyeglass stems as I walk from the windows which front Beacon Street to the rear wall of the room. I am carrying the journal which I've rolled into a tube. The paper is slick and expensive. The pages are filled with the dissembled panic of professors who are writing, writing, all over this country and saying nothing at all. I suppose I have to eat soon. I'm not hungry. What I'm thinking about is the untracked snow lying upon the slope behind the house I lived in as a boy. I inhale deeply as though I were outside on a clear cold day instead of inside this room with its close smell of my life.

"It's not people I remember. Only places. How I miss my senses! And I'm confounded by this *thing* in me that continues to live, to gather impressions, to crave, if infrequently, its supper. Do you ever wonder about the past? I mean—regard it with wonder? Do you like your work? How is your life?"

Gerald put down the page and began to type.

"You ask me if I like my work," he wrote. "To be frank, I don't think about it. It's what I do. Fund-raising has its tedium, although I do get an occasional trip from it. But doesn't everything have tedium. I seem to have a flair for what I do. My family often suggests they could use my talent on the homefront. Ha-ha. Still, we manage. Of course, I think about things, too. But there's no point in brooding, is there? Although at our age, I suppose we're more susceptible to it. After all, the choices we have thin out, don't they? Incidentally, you don't mention a family. Have you one? Children?"

He considered the last few sentences. They were too personal: they might provoke intimate revelations he had no interest in.

When Jack's first letter followed his Boston trip by a few days, he had been surprised. He hadn't been sure Jack would remember him, much less track down his address and start writing to him. When Gerald had discovered his phone number in the Boston directory and dialed it, he had found that Jack was living in a residential club. He had been relieved Jack wasn't in. The impulse to call him had been fleeting.

Jack had been "grieved" to miss his call, he had written in his first long letter. It included a lengthy description of Jack's vacation in Greece last summer. Gerald had skipped most of that. The word "grieved" made him uneasy. He felt obliged to reply. He had written a brief note, asking Jack if he ever saw any of their old classmates from the Boston school they had both gone to. About himself, he wrote only that he had one son who was in college, that he enjoyed living in New York and that he raised funds for an adoption agency.

And now this second letter had arrived from Jack with its intimacies and speculations. He picked up the last of the sheets and read it through.

"Yesterday," Jack had written, "I left my office to go to my sophomore class. On the way there, I forgot completely what I had intended to lecture on. Forgot everything! Even where I was! I felt faint and I stretched out my hands to support myself on the walls of the corridor. Of course I couldn't reach them both at once so I bobbled from side to side. I was staggering along in this fashion when I met the chairman of my department on his way home, as I learned later, because of a viral attack. He held up his briefcase in such a way that I couldn't get past him. He seemed enraged! I couldn't explain why I was feeling the walls like a giant fly. I couldn't speak at all! I lowered my arms. He lowered his briefcase, and we went our separate ways. I recalled what I was to lecture on, and he, I suppose, went home. It was an intense confrontation. Why was he so angry? How can I explain my muteness? Shouldn't I write him a note?"

Jack had ended the letter then with only his name. Irritably, Gerald struck at the keys of his typewriter.

"Jack," he wrote, "you must not get so stuck in incidents that mean nothing. We all have these flurries of confusion. One must simply stick to one's purpose. The obvious explanation for the situation you described is that your chairman was ill and wanted to get home in a hurry. Can you have forgotten that your arms were stretched out as though to prevent him from passing you? Think how it may have appeared to him. I'm making more of this trivial incident than it merits only in order to suggest that what was so strange about it was that a simple explanation didn't occur to you instantly."

Gerald took the page out of the machine and inked out the questions about Jack's family life. He inserted another page.

"That's a long letter," observed his wife who put a cup of tea for him on the table.

"It's double-spaced," he said.

As children, Jack and he had been more or less friendly in school. They had often gone to the movies on Saturday afternoons when Gerald had enough money to pay for his ticket. Gerald had sometimes visited Jack's house.

Jack's family had been well-off. He had lived in a big house with white clapboard siding. At the front there was a well-tended lawn with hedges and flowering shrubs, and in the back, a narrow meadow on the slope of a hill where the family kept a saddle horse which Gerald had been told he couldn't ride. Recollecting now his fear of animals in those days, he laughed to think how humiliated he'd been by Mrs. Crowder's admonition concerning that lousy horse. He wouldn't have ridden a saddled rabbit in those days.

Gerald's family had lived in the more deteriorated half of a two-family dwelling. Because the walls had been thin, Gerald in remembering the house was not sure he was recalling his parents' quarrels or the neighbors'.

He began a new sentence.

"After all," he wrote, "your life can't have been so tough. I recall your house quite well. You had a window seat in your bedroom and a horse of your own in a meadow."

He read over what he had written, noting that his last sentences were inconsonant with what had preceded them. He was suddenly bored.

Beverly called him to come to the bedroom and watch

television. A comedian they both liked was defending ethnic humor on a panel discussion. He didn't write anymore that evening.

The next morning before leaving for his office, he finished the letter hurriedly. He wrote:

"Work piles up at this time of year. Our spring drive is on. You can imagine how little time I have for such relaxations as writing to an old acquaintance. It was nice to hear from you."

He mailed the letter in the apartment house slot and forgot about it. A reply came within a few days. Beverly had left it on his plate as though it was his dinner.

"I managed to decipher your inked out lines," it began. "I was most interested in what you would cross out. But somewhat disappointed at your question. I have had several families. I have three children. I'm alone now.

"About the incident with my chairman. I want to tell you that it's the instant explanation you suggest that I want to resist. All my life, I've rushed to explain things within the second, like an addict grabbing up a narcotic. My two divorces for instance."

"All his life," Gerald said aloud. "For God's sake . . . all anyone's life . . ." He looked up and across the table at Beverly. "He irritates me," he said.

"After that letter arrived this morning," she began, "I found the other two on your night table. I read them."

"You did?" he asked, surprised. "I thought I'd thrown them out. I can see myself throwing them in the garbage."

"Why don't you do that now? Throw them all out?"

"Yes . . . but I'll finish this one. Then I'll put a stop to the whole thing."

After supper, Gerald went back to Jack's letter.

"I fear you think I'm looking for a companion in misery. I'm not," the letter continued. "It's because we are, as you said, old acquaintances, that I write you now. My friends and I are used to each other. There's something else, too. You're the only person I know from my true past, my childhood. Perhaps that's the main thing. When I found your message here at my club, my heart began to pound! It was nearly like the excitement of hope. I don't know what about. But there it is. And I can't tell my friends I don't understand anything. Money, for example. Sex. Death. What is goodness?

"One of my students came to my office to tell me she was in love with me and couldn't concentrate on the course work. She said my face was so interesting. Interesting! I insisted she turn in her overdue term paper. She burst into tears. Later, I was so distressed, I cancelled a dinner engagement and went home and made myself sick drinking brandy.

"I've been trying to finish a piece on Andrew Marvell. It's simply not worth finishing. I thought of having the girl transferred to another section. Maybe I should suggest marriage to her, steal her away from the young men. That girl shouldn't be in college. She wants to live! Do you remember what that means to an eighteen-year-old?

"Are you well-off? What's your wife like? Have you had just one wife?"

Gerald put down the letter. "He's insulting," he said. "He knew how to be patronizing when he was a kid."

"I wonder why you called him in the first place," Beverly said. Gerald was bothered by a note of sadness in her voice. It was as though some sorrow from an unknown source were reaching out to touch them both.

Later on, he replied to Jack's letter.

"Jack, you are too self-involved. Don't you realize I might find some of your questions offensive? Why the hell did you end up living alone in some crummy residential club? You write as though a decent place to live is nothing. Did you ever trouble yourself to come to *my* house when we were kids? No. You *knew* you had everything. What are you complaining about? What's wrong with being a teacher? You think you've been singled out for special suffering? Look around you! Why *should* that girl care about *Beowulf,* or whatever dead stuff she's supposed to read in your course? You're damned right, she wants to live!"

That night Gerald lay awake in the dark, his hands clasped behind his neck, staring up at the ceiling. He tried to recall with great particularity what Jack had looked like. It had been over thirty-five years since they had last seen each other. All he could recall was a round face and pale eyes above the collar of a navy blue coat. The only detail that occurred to him was the way the coat buttons were so tightly sewn on. His own jacket was always scarred by the jagged tears where his buttons had been.

An answer came by return mail. Gerald opened the letter with dread. "Yes!" Jack began without his usual greeting. "That's what I wanted! What a good letter! Now I'm beginning to remember you. And other things. Who was it made you wear those black stockings? I especially noticed them when you bent over to make a snowball. I think I must have made some snotty remark about them because it seems to me you got very angry. Do you recall?

The sky was nearly black, probably January. The snow had been on the ground for days. We were in the schoolyard. The janitor had scattered cinders all around. You and I were the only children there. You were shivering. Those bitter cold days! Do you remember Miss Hamilton who taught 3rd grade? Do you remember Janet Lee who had little breasts when all the rest of us could hardly tell male from female? Janet wore a locket. By the way, I don't teach *Beowulf.* I'm really glad we're making this connection. It helps me to think."

"He's going to drive me crazy," said Gerald. Beverly was standing in front of him, her coat on, ready to leave for the theater.

"We'll be late," she said.

"I don't know," he said. "I just don't know. Why don't you sit down here next to me? Do we have to go see that play? Couldn't we give away the tickets?"

"You mustn't let him do this to us," she said. "Don't answer him anymore."

When they got home that night, Gerald wrote his son a long letter. He described the house he had lived in as a child, and the quarrels he had heard on both sides of the thin walls. He described Janet Lee whom, up to now, he had long forgotten. He even remembered whose picture Janet had carried in her locket—a baby snapshot of herself. He didn't write to Jack.

Several weeks passed with no word from Boston. Then a postcard arrived. It read: "I'll be in New York the evening of April 23rd. I have to give a lecture. Hope you can spare me an hour. I'll be returning to Boston on the last shuttle so it will be the briefest of visits."

"I won't see him," said Gerald.

"What are you going to do?" Beverly asked. "Tomorrow is the twenty-third."

"He did it on purpose, not giving me time to write him back."

"You can phone," she said.

"I won't do it," he said loudly. "I won't let him *make* me do anything. He takes his chances. It's his lookout. He should have called *me*, after all."

"But if he's coming all this way . . ."

"Bev, you're so contrary. He's coming to the city to give a lecture. These professors and their lectures . . ."

She looked baffled.

Gerald watched a late movie on television. He was thinking about what he was going to do, and he felt badly about it. But he knew himself. He didn't want to see Jack and he wasn't going to. What was significant about his first twelve years was that he had survived them. He didn't need anyone from that time of his life to remind him of what it had been like.

The following evening, they left a note scotch-taped to the front door saying they had a sudden emergency and had had to go out. Beverly hesitated as they stood in the hall, waiting for the elevator, then she asked Gerald if they couldn't expand the note somewhat. It looked so scant.

"It doesn't matter what I write," Gerald said. "He'll get the point."

"I feel sorry for him," she said softly.

"Don't," he said, and gripped her arm strongly as the elevator door opened.

They stayed out until one in the morning. For an hour after the movie they had seen, they sat in a coffee shop on 57th Street, sharing a pastry, looking through the paperback books they had bought in a nearby store. Then they walked home through a light rain.

Jack's answer had been slipped under the door. Gerald picked it up but didn't look at it. Then, as Beverly stood in front of the dresser mirror removing hairpins, he read it.

"I'm sorry," it began. "But I see. I understand. After all, what did we have in common except blind hopes?" It was signed with the initial *J* as though, Gerald thought, he had been too disheartened to write out his name.

"Well, what do you think?" he asked, handing Beverly the note. He glimpsed on its back the message he had left for Jack. The brief sentence, the word *emergency*, looked stern and powerful to him.

"It'll be finished now, I guess," she said.

"We didn't have *anything* in common," Gerald said. "Not one thing!" His voice grew louder. "Blind hopes . . . a rich little bastard like that with his buttons sewed on for life!"

He bent suddenly to untie his shoelaces. The muscles of his back tightened. Instead of the lisle hose he was wearing, he felt once again around his ankles the wet thickness of black wool stockings, and in his empty hands, he felt the hard, cinder-packed snow as he shaped it with his freezing palms. Raising his head quickly to sight the boy walking away from him in a navy blue coat, he brought his arm up in an arc and threw the snowball past his wife standing there in front of her mirror, staring at him, past the beige walls of the bedroom, at the retreating back, seeing just beyond it the dark winter sky, and joyously breathing in a great draught of the cinder-smelling arctic air, as the boy he struck so unerringly cried out in pain.

THE LIVING

AFTER THE FUNERAL, we stood around awhile on the street corner right near the funeral parlor. There was a lot of vegetables in crates sitting out in front of a grocery store and I couldn't help my eyes sliding over to those big purple bananas that the Puerto Ricans buy. Flies was buzzing over everything, but those purple bananas wasn't even sweating like the other fruit, flies didn't bother them, they lay there looking like they was in a cold cellar. They made me feel bad and I don't know why.

My wife—I don't live with her no more but we still married—she was crying and mopping up her face and pulling at her dress because she was so hot. I couldn't stop myself from seeing she was getting fat, especially in her shoulders. Why do I have to notice so much? Sometimes I wish I was a little like her, holler when things are bad, and laugh when it's okay. But not me. I'm always seeing the things that are all around what I should be paying attention to. Like when I go for a job, I'm watching the man's face, seeing how his teeth fit in his jaws, what his shirt cuffs look like and what he's got on his desk, instead of asking him where and how much and how long.

My wife calls Curtis the "little baby." I don't understand why she thinks he's so little. He is old enough to be buried in his cadet suit.

Quite a few people came to the funeral, mostly neighbors, I guess. Even my brother came. I haven't seen him for eight years, and after he looked at Curtis lying in the coffin, he remarked how big he'd grown. But then the last time he'd seen Curtis was just a few months after he'd been born when we were still living in Brooklyn before we moved uptown.

"What are you looking at those vegetables for when you should be thinking about your dead baby!" my wife cried. And Yvonne, who is ten now, started howling and grabbed my wife around her middle. Yvonne looked very neat, I noticed, and her shoes were all polished up. I hadn't seen her for a long time. I used to go by and visit them, but my wife and I always had to have our fight, and it got so the children would just go out of the room to get away, so I hardly ever had a chance to talk to them.

"What good is thinking about him going to do him now?" I asked her. "You should of thought about him when you let him go up to the roof all the time just so you could be alone to work yourself all up about what a mean bastard I was and how bad I did you!" She began to yell and moan. I couldn't even make out what she was saying. I started wondering how they got Curtis to look so nice when he had fallen four stories to the street. Then the grocer came out and waved his hands at us and shouted in Spanish, calling us names probably.

Most of the people who had come to the funeral had gone off down the street. My brother was standing in front of the funeral parlor and talking to Light Marsh, who is my wife's cousin. I don't know why *he* came to Curtis' funeral. That's a man who's hardly interested in anything living or dead except his car. But he was going to drive us out to the cemetery so I didn't make my usual remarks about him.

It was a terrible hot drive. Light all the time talking about these gadgets he's got for his Caddie and pointing at them with his long finger and driving with the other hand, while my wife carried on in her corner. My brother kept grinning at Light and then turning around to look sad at me. Yvonne rested herself against my ribs and I patted her head and felt sorrier for her than I did for anybody else. Suddenly she looked up while Light and my brother were arguing about which was the fastest way to the cemetery.

"Why did they have that doll in the window?" she asked me. At first, I didn't know what she meant. Then I remembered that in the funeral parlor window, on a shelf, there had been this plastic doll held upright by some kind of metal prong and the doll had a crown and was wearing some kind of lace cape. When I first walked in, I had noticed how dusty the shelf was and how the crown looked like it was made out of a silver candy wrapper.

"I don't know," I answered.

"Isn't it supposed to be for dead people? Why they get that doll then?" she whispered.

"Maybe she's supposed to be a saint or something like that," I said.

"Don't tell her none of your lies," my wife said.

Light had begun to talk about the war and this country and how crazy everything was getting and what hard times were coming, and I laughed. "Hard times *coming?*" I said. "What I want to know is, when are they *going?*"

"You ought to get into a steady business," my brother said. I think he's been saying that since I was three and he was five.

"You mean, like the numbers?" I asked.

"Why don't you go to school and take up something," he asked. "You ought to grab what's there."

"He know all about grabbing," said my wife.

"Did it hurt Curtis?" Yvonne asked.

All of a sudden, I got scared, sitting in that big white car that probably had thirty-six payments left on it, with my brother all shut into his best suit and my wife getting fatter every minute, and Light Marsh telling me all about the world and Yvonne asking me questions like I was supposed to know everything.

"No, baby, no, it couldna hurt him," my wife said. "He didn't know what hit him."

"The ground hit him," Yvonne said, and sat up straight.

Then, pretty soon, Yvonne starts out with "Daddy—" but we was there, and I got busy getting out of the car. I'll never know what she was going to ask me, maybe, who the hell was I anyhow?

Some of the people who had been at the parlor had got there their own way, and they were standing near the hole with the preacher. His head was bowed and sweat was running down his forehead.

They had this carpet, maybe five feet by five, made out of stuff that was supposed to look like grass, and it was spread over the dirt they had dug out of Curtis' grave. There were so many gravestones sticking up out of the ground, you wouldn't think there was room for one more child.

The coffin was closed up now. It had a sling around it so it could be lowered into the ground. There were two men standing a few yards away, leaning on shovels. Gravediggers, I guess. They were wearing caps and work clothes. They didn't have any expression at all on their faces, but even so I thought they was laughing at us. Maybe it's because I figure colored people is funny to white people whether they're dead or alive. I had this picture of myself—it was so fast I hardly saw it—of me lifting up one of those shovels and bashing their heads in.

They threw some dirt on Curtis and lowered him and I heard the preacher's voice getting louder, but I couldn't get any sense out of what he was saying. The graveyard stretched further than I could see. I heard cars so I knew there must be big highways all around.

Light said he'd drive us back to the parlor. My brother went off with some man who was going his way. He shook my hand before he left and told me not to feel too bad. And I said, yeah, I'd try not to.

Light showed off all the way back, asking Yvonne would she like a doll and telling me to drop around, he'd get me a good job, and asking how we was paying for all this funeral expense. I didn't want to talk about that. I gave my wife the thirty-eight dollars I had, and she must have got the rest somewhere, maybe from her daddy who runs an elevator in an apartment building downtown, and has a little house with a yard in the Bronx. I don't know why he didn't come to Curtis' funeral, maybe because he knew I'd be there.

We got out of the car in front of the grocery store. My wife wasn't crying anymore but she looked awful. Her hat was coming down the back of her head, and her eyes looked big and starey.

"You want to go to a movie?" I asked.

"What is the matter with you," she said.

"Yeah, Daddy. Can we go?" Yvonne asked.

"Well . . . I thought it would be better, so you don't have to go back home right now. There's a Loew's right up here near by."

She was looking at me, but I was looking over her shoulder. There were fewer bananas in the box now. Somebody must have been buying them while we were out putting Curtis in the ground.

"Don't you feel *bad*?" she asked like she'd been thinking hard to find the thing to say that would straighten me out.

"I feel bad," I said.

Then we all started to walk up the block, and pretty soon we came to the movie. I didn't look to see what was playing.

It was cool inside, that big black coolness I've always liked about movies. Hardly anybody was in there, a few people with nothing to do, getting out of the sun.

I bought Yvonne some peanuts and she settled back in her seat. My wife took off her hat and sank down and rested her head. They were showing a cartoon. It didn't look so good on that big screen. The animals had those faces that don't look like anything living or dead, and the voices they put in them were screaming and laughing and hooting so loud it made me hunch down in the seat.

I don't know . . . but I think there's nothing worse than that, nothing sadder anyhow, than a movie on a hot weekday afternoon with maybe a dozen people sprinkled around, watching a cartoon that's supposed to be for children.

I began to feel so bad sitting there, looking at my wife's and Yvonne's faces in the light from the screen, then looking back at the cartoon and seeing some goddamn big mouse in a cape running along the floor, that I could've yelled.

And then I did yell. My wife and Yvonne grabbed me up out of the seat and took me up the aisle and I was yelling all the time, thinking of how the street would be, of those sweating, rotting vegetables at the grocer's, and that plastic doll, and Light Marsh in his white man's car, and Curtis dead and dressed up like he was going to war, and the man I had to see tomorrow about a job sorting packages. None of it mattered, not even my yelling mattered.

We were all gone, not just Curtis, but Yvonne, my wife and me, gone, gone, gone . . .

LORD RANDAL

TAKE THE FIRST STEP. They said my child is laying down there, one foot, they say, half stuck in a bag of garbage like he had crawled out of it. Black beans and candy wrappers, bones, rags and coffee grounds, and Robert Brown on the stoop.

This street in the morning looks like a burnt mattress after the firemen put the fire out. The children burst out of the doors like black seed pods and they take all that glass—is it my window that broke?—and all those bottles and they smash them up after school when the street is done smoking and stinking. The children make knives from the busted springs and jump out—Bam!—from the doors. I say—whoosh!—and they run away. With the springs and the glass they got plenty to do all day after school.

On this floor Mrs. Perez is shouting and hollering. She say, "Ay! Ay!," and I say she should go back wherever she come from.

Back there her husband, or whatever, could chase her through all that brush they got down there. He could mash her up where the pigs is. But here on this floor in that room with four walls and a window and a door, he got no right. I got to listen to *that* all night? She got yellow skin where he hits. And she grin at me like she won something. I see from here the snow is coming. That's right, fall down baby, cover it all up.

I take the second step. Robert Brown is a smart boy and I don't think he's anything but drunk down there. He likes coffee black, he likes his cuffs clean and he robbed me from my pocketbook but he never drank before. Now then he got that little car, German. But where did they get the money? Where do they get all the money from when in my life you never could see that kind of sugar? My sister's boy he had money too and he was hooked when he was almost a baby and they got him and sent him to the place and he come back and got hooked again and now he lay around on the couch all day and look tired.

But Robert Brown is nobody's fool. He see them all around here on this street sleepy and scratching theyselves all the long day and leaning up against nothing. He laugh. He says, "Look at the fools, mamma!" But I don't even look.

Here is Gloria screaming again. Last summer she was throwing herself around in a pink hoop and now she got Louie. She's standing there so mad, she's rocking, and she's calling him names and shaking her little butt. Is she mad? Or what? He say, "No peace around here at all," and he walk off and she laugh now, "Ha, ha, ha."

But then I never seen anything like the way after a woman tells a man to get out, how she looks when he goes and stand there saying, "Ha, ha, ha," and he don't turn around, he walk up the street with his cap just so, his hands in his pocket and don't turn around. There she is pretending she got her own business too and when he is far from her sight, she take off after him, walking fast like him, and still shaking with it. Gloria going to find out now: If you tell them to go, they go.

I take the third step. Willie Prentice in his life got himself cut six ways and he's fixing up to fight again. I see that Portorican grinding his teeth and they are going to cut each other right here in the hall. Now, they're just looking, head turning, right, left, slow, getting ready. But the Portorican is going to scream pretty soon like a buzzsaw.

Knives. When Buddy was little and he cut his toe with the axe, our daddy poured kerosene into the cut and took ashes from the stove and poured them over that toe and bound it up with flannel and he got well.

We stole too from my daddy—sewed up eggs in the hems of our coat and went down the road to school and stopped by the store and traded those eggs for stockings and candy.

On Monday we washed, on Tuesday we ironed, on Wednesday we scrubbed the floor with potash, on Thursday we run off and did what we did.

My little brother Buddy, he threw a turtle in the fire once and it walked clean out of its shell but Robert Brown never hurt the cats around here. And he took care of that dog till it run off. He went to school and learned what he had to and he went to the store and sometimes he polished his own shoes and he watched all the fighting around here and never said nothing and he never went up on the roof with the rest of them to do what they do up there and he never stole from nobody but me. Once he asked me why *they* come around sometime and I didn't tell him they looking for colored tail or the stuff. I said they was policemen checking up. He say, "Checking up on what?" And I say the city got all these policemen and they got to do something with them.

I take the fourth step. The old women are crowding up on me. They step when I step—and I go slow. I don't believe Robert Brown got into a fight. He is too fast a boy. And he never got mixed up with nobody around here. No. He say he got his own friends. Then he brought her around. He say, "This is my mamma," and she say, "Hello, Mrs. Brown." But did she mean Mrs. Brown? She never been in a place like this before I could see and she grin all the time and she was with him like white on rice, stuck on him, grabbing him, taking him.

I say what do you want Robert with a young white girl like that and he say, "Time has changed, mamma." He say, "I got friends, mamma." And I say, "She got friends too and maybe they aren't your friends."

She bring me bacon once, and flowers. Why did she do that? She think I don't know anything but bacon? Get away old women! I go down by myself and don't catch hold of my arm because I throw you all down the rest of the stairs. I throw you into the street. And they didn't see the blood with their own eyes so how they know it is there?

I take the fifth step. He take her around in that little car and he wear a white scarf and he shoot out his cuffs like he had to go someplace to learn to do it. I told him to be careful and he say I got to learn. What did I mean and what do he mean?

They are crowding up in front of me now but I can't hear what they say because the city is taking up the garbage which they do ten times a day and ten times a night. Where do we get all this garbage from? They crowding up there in front of me but I see Whitey got a bottle of Texas rum in his back pocket and George he is going to lift it right out like it was a straight splinter. They are all looking down at the stoop. I push them away easy because they made of sticks. They weak.

I can see him. He's laying there and his foot is half stuck in a bag of garbage like they said. Is he drunk?

Because I don't see that blood. Robert Brown—Robert Brown— Are you drunk, boy?

ACKNOWLEDGMENTS

"Lord Randal" first published in *The Negro Digest*, July 1965.

"The Living" first published in *The Negro Digest*, September/
October 1968.

"Sitting Down and Alone" first published in *Confrontation*, Fall/
Winter 1978.

"News from the World" first published in *Short Shorts*, ed. Irving
and Ilana Howe (David Godine, 1982).

"By the Sea" first published in *The Threepenny Review*, 1986.

"Other Places" first published in *The Horn Book Magazine*,
January/February 1987.

"Unquestioned Answers" first published in *The Zena Sutherland
Lectures, 1983–1992*, ed. Betsy Hearne (Clarion Books, 1993).

"The Stop of Truth" first published in *Censored Books: Critical*

Viewpoints, ed. Lee Burress, Nicholas J. Karolides, and John M. Kean (Scarecrow Press, 1995).

"Grace" first published in *Harper's*, June 2003.

"The Broad Estates of Death" first published in *Harper's*, April 2004.

"Way Down Yonder" first published in *Lire*, December 2005.

"Franchot Tone at the Paramount" first published in *Playboy*, December 2007.

"Frieda in Taos" first published in *The Yale Review*, Spring 2008.

"The Tender Night" first published in *The Paris Review*, Summer 2008.

"Light on the Dark Side" first published in *The New York Review of Books*, December 2, 2009.

"Clem" first published in *The Yale Review*, Spring 2010.